THE STAMP OF HOOF, THE STROKE OF AXE . . .

Bili mindspoke Mahvros, "Be ready to fight, brother!" The huge black horse quickened his gait in response to Bili's command, raised his head and voiced a shrill, equine challenge, and then bore down on his promised victims.

The leading attacker held up his shield to fend off Bili's axe, while he aimed a hacking cut at Mahvros' thick neck. The stout target crumpled like wet paper and the axeblade bit completely through and deep into the arm beneath, the force of the buffet hurling the man down to a singularly messy death amid the stamping hooves.

But Bili failed to see the man who galloped in from his left, and then a hardflung throwingaxe caromed off Bili's helm, nearly deafening him and filling his head full of a tight red-blackness shot with dazzling white stars . . .

Also by Robert Adams in the *Horseclans* series publshed by Futura

THE COMING OF THE HORSECLANS
SWORDS OF THE HORSECLANS

ROBERT ADAMS

Revenge of the Horseclans

A Horseclans Novel

Futura

An Orbit Book

HORSECLANS No. 3: *Revenge of the Horseclans* by Robert Adams

This edition published in 1984 by
Futura Publications, a Division of
Macdonald & Co (Publishers) Ltd
London & Sydney
Reprinted 1984

ISBN 0 7088 8125 4

Printed and bound in Great Britain by
Hazell Watson & Viney Limited,
Member of the BPCC Group,
Aylesbury, Bucks

Futura Publications
A Division of
Macdonald & Co (Publishers) Ltd
Maxwell House
74 Worship Street
London EC2A 2EN
A BPCC plc Company

For Dr. Isaac Asimov, whose prodigious talents and proclivities are so widely renowned; for Cherry and Jack Weiner; for Susan Schwartz and the Koala Bear; for John Estren and Tom Anderson; for two of the finest young ladies in fandom, Claire Eddy and Sally Ann Steg

Oh, sing me of Morguhn, the brave, true, and strong.
Yes, sing me of Morguhn and let the song be long.
Sing of the Red Eagle that leads on to fame.
Sing of the mighty Morguhns, by deed and by name.
A Morguhn, A Morguhn,
A Morguhn, the shout,
While sharp Morguhn steel
Every foeman does rout.
Oh, lead on, Red Eagle, to glory or to Wind,
As you led those doughty Morguhns, from whom we descend.

—*ancient warsong of Clan Morguhn.*

REVENGE OF THE HORSECLANS

PROLOGUE

No matter how carefully Sir Bili Morguhn rearranged his hooded cloak, the cold, driving rain continued to find a sure path into his already sodden brigandine. Wearily, he leaned forward as his plodding gelding commenced to ascend yet another hill, and the movement started his nose to dripping again. Bili resignedly employed gauntleted fingers to blow some of the drip from his reddened nostrils, then vainly searched his person for a dry bit of cloth with which to wipe them. Leaning back against the high cantle as the gelding gingerly negotiated the mud-slick downgrade of the Traderoad, he thought that he could feel his every joint creak in harmony with his saddle. A reverie of the broad, sundappled meadows of his patrimonial estates flitted through his mind.

The wet hide of his stallion's massive barrel came to rest against his booted leg and the warhorse mindspoke him, "Mahvros, too, thinks of the land loved by Sun and Wind, and he wishes now but a single roll in soft, *dry* grass. Is it many more days of wet and cold until we be there?"

Bili sighed in sympathy. "It's considered to be a two-week journey by the traders," he answered telepathically. "But I hope to make it in ten days . . . less, if possible, despite this abominable weather. That's why I bought the geldings and the mule; you're too good a friend to risk foundering."

While speaking he reached over and patted the

muscle-corded withers, then ran his hand up to the crest and gently kneaded the thick neck. Could the big black have purred, he would have then. As it was, he beamed a wordless reaffirmation of his lifelong love for and devotion to Bili. Between the two minds, human and equine, flowed a depthless stream of mutual respect and trust and friendship.

The gelding raised his drooping head briefly and snorted. In his turn, Mahvros arched his neck and snorted in reply. The gelding, eyes rolling, shied from the stallion's threat, stumbled in the rock-studded mud, and all but fell. Only Bili's superb horsemanship kept him in his seat and the gelding on his feet. He was about to chide Mahvros, who knew that the newly acquired animals were terrified of him, when the warhorse again mindspoke.

"Best to sit me, now, Brother. Stallions ahead, and mares and sexless ones and many mules. Their riders fight." There were eager undertones in the big horse's mindspeak, for he loved a fight.

A bare week ago, Bili might have been every bit as eager, but now, with his need to speedily complete his journey pressing upon him, he could see only the delay which a skirmish might entail. Nonetheless, he reined the gelding onto the shoulder where the mud was not so deep, then dismounted, tethered the two hacks and the mule, and mounted the monstrous black stallion.

Once in the familiar war kak, he removed the cloak and draped it over the mule's packsaddle, then unslung his small, heavyweight target and strapped it on his left arm. While Mahvros quivered with joyful anticipation, Bili uncased his huge axe and tightened its thong on his right wrist. Lastly, he slid into place his helm's nasal and snapped down the cheekpieces.

"All right, Brother," he mindspoke the stamping stallion. "Let us see what lies ahead . . . but *quietly*, mind you! And charge only if I so command."

For all his bulk, Mahvros was capable of moving silently as a cat. But even a cat would have found creeping difficult on the mudsucking road, so Bili put his mount to the wooded slope which flanked it. At the crest he was glad he had exercised elementary caution, for where the road curved around the hill sat two horsemen with bared blades.

Just below his hilltop position, a hot little fight was in progress round about a stonewalled travelers' spring and six huge traderwagons. The attackers were obviously brigands rather than troopers, such that had become all too common along the lonelier stretches of the traderoads, since King Gilbuht had stripped away the bulk of the usual patrols to augment his cavalry in the current war.

The defenders, fighting heavy odds, included a few Freefighters—Rahdzburkers, from the look of them—and a few more hastily armed merchants, ebonskinned men garbed in the style of the Kahleefait of Zahrtohgah. That the tiny force were no mean warriors was attested by the dozen or so still or twitching brigands who were scattered about the ground before them. Even as he watched, a helmeted merchant fitted a broadbladed dart to a throwing-stick and sent a hefty robber crashing into the mud, thick fingers clawing at the steel sunk deep in his chest. But in the same time, a Freefighter and two merchants were hacked to earth. The defenders were fighting a lost battle; the odds were just too heavy to allow of aught but defeat and death for the doughty little band. Unless . . .

Bili's thoughts raced. Not all the normal patrols were gone from this part of the Kingdom of Harzburk, but they no longer rode on any sort of schedule, for they had too much ground to cover with too few men. Therefore, these bandits were taking a considerable risk to attack a merchant train in broad daylight; that must be the reason for the roadguards below the hill.

Grinning with the seed of a chancy plan, he backed

Mahvros a little way back into the woods, then lifted to his lips his silver-mounted bullshorn. Filling his lungs, he sounded the familiar call, then again and a third time.

Hefting his axe, he next gave Mahvros the signal to charge, adding, "Make much noise, Brother, as much as a half troop of dragoons!"

Then it was over the crest and out of the woods and barrelling down the steep slope toward the raging battle. The stallion's hooves were a bass thunder through the swirling groundmist.

Raising his heavy axe and whirling it over his head, Bili shouted, *"UP, UP HARZBURK! UP HARZBURK!* FIRST SQUAD LEFT! FOURTH SQUAD RIGHT! ARCHERS TO THE FLANKS! *UP HARZBURK!"*

From below came a confused babble of shouts, then one cracked tenor rang above the rest, ". . . git t'hell outa here! That there's Sir Hinree's Troop, I reca'nize his black horse!"

Then Bili found himself among a milling cluster of brigands. A shaggy pony went down, bowled over by Mahvros's impetus, and the savage warhorse went at the downed animal and man with teeth and hooves. Bili laid about him with the doublebitted axe, parrying swords on its steel shaft and emptying saddle after saddle. All at once, there were no riders before him, only a couple of groaning, dying bandits on the ground.

The opaque mist which had so far been but patches had thickened and coalesced since he had launched his reckless charge. He almost axed an unmounted man who appeared on his right, before he recognized the armor and gear of a Rahdzburker Freefighter. The stranger stopped long enough to dispatch a wounded brigand, then limped smiling up to Bili.

"I never thought I'd be glad to hear the Harzburker warcry, my lord, not after Behreesburk; but by the Sacred Sword, you and your troop could not have been better come! But . . ." He glanced about him bewilderedly. ". . . where *is* your troop, sir?"

Showing every tooth, Bili chuckled, "You're looking at it, Freefighter. I be no patrol, only a traveler like your employer."

CHAPTER I

Aside from rare border raids, there had been no real warfare within the boundaries of Bili Morguhn's homeland for nigh a hundred years, though its armies and fleets were seldom idle. Many hostile peoples pressed upon its borders and the sea-lanes required constant patrolling. The Confederation, toward which he rode in such haste, was the largest principality in all the known lands. Despite the Traderoads—which were much better maintained there than in other lands—months were necessary for traders to travel from one end of the Confederation to the other. Even messengers of the High-Lord, who sometimes covered a hundred miles in a day, could not go from end to end in much under fifteen days.

As a consequence, news was always late, and life moved slowly and unhurriedly away from the capital of the Confederation or the port cities or the archducal capitals. The Duchy of Morguhn was no exception; the peace and ordered tranquility well-suited the father of Bili and his eight brothers, giving him the time needed to devote himself exclusively to his lands and his books.

Prior to the death of Bili's grandfather, Hwahruhn Morguhn had soldiered up and down the Middle Kingdoms with a troop of Kindred noblemen under the command of his kinsman, Djeen Morguhn. Djeen—who had gone on to rise swiftly to the rank of Strahteegos in the Army of the Confederation—and Hwahruhn had both distinguished themselves at the seige of Kooleezburk. After its conclusion, Hwahruhn had wed the daughters of the victor, Duke Tchahrlz of Zunburk, sending his new brides south to dwell with his father, while Djeen marched the troop off on a new campaign.

As the two lovely girls and their escort wended their way through Kehnooryos Ehlahs, capital province of the Confederation, a band of Morguhn men spurred tired horses northward, to bear word to Hwahruhn of his father's death.

Confirmed Thoheeks and Chief Morguhn of Morguhn, Hwahruhn had settled down with his young brides—Mahrnee, fourteen, and Behrnees, fifteen—to commence the siring of legitimate sons to succeed him. It had been a very late marriage; Hwahruhn was over thirty-five years of age.

Within the next six years his blond wives presented him with eleven sons. The fact that nine of these sons still lived at the time of Bili's ride was considered amazing. For despite the best efforts of the High-Lord to improve the sanitation of cities and towns, despite his importation of skilled physicians from the Black Kingdoms, despite his establishment of a school in the capital to train Ehleenoee physicians in more advanced and antiseptic techniques, disease still ran high in the Confederation, taking off the young and the old.

In most provinces, few Kindred nobles—descendants of the Horseclansmen who had received lands from the Undying High-Lord—dwelt in the unhealthy environs of their cities, preferring instead their halls amid their ranches and farms. So it was in spacious, sunny Morguhn Hall that Bili was born and it was there that he remained throughout his first eight years of life.

He never needed to be taught to mindspeak, communicating thus long ere he learned vocal communication; nor was it needful to teach him to ride. His uncles and mothers were mightily pleased at these innate abilities, as was too his father in his quiet way.

By the time the lad was eight, his father had granted grudging permission that his heir be given to the care of his mothers' cousin, Gilbuht, King of Harzburk, for education, wartraining, and gentlemanly polish. Those years of residence at the Iron King's bloodspattered court—riddled with intrigues which kept the Royal torturers and executioners busy—and service with the standing army of tough, practical younger sons and mercenaries molded the gangling, big-boned boy into the broadshouldered, steel-thewed man Bili had become by his sixteenth year. Most of his mentors, noble and Freefighter alike, could be cruel, rapacious, and frighteningly coldblooded toward their foes; but they were generally honest in dealing with their comrades and strictly honorable within their code.

Three months prior to Bili's eighteenth summer, his father was struck down by a sudden paralysis, and his mothers sent word for him to return, indicating that speed was essential, since his father might not live long. King Gilbuht freely offered him a strong escort, but knowing that a troop would slow him, he elected to ride alone.

Despite rain, sleet, mud, the brief skirmish, and other assorted difficulties, Bili, Mahvros and the mule arrived at Morguhn Hall but nine days after they had departed King Gilbuht's capital. Only his mothers recognized the tall, hard, weather-darkened warrior who, stubblefaced and travelstained, strode stiffleggedly out of the night and into the hall.

But Hwahruhn clung to life and, hearing of his illness, the *Ahrkeethoheeks* Petros sent a master physician to tend him. Under the skillful care of Master Ahlee and his apprentice, the *Thoheeks* made a slow but halting improvement. As the planting season passed, he regained limited use of his left arm and some sensation in his left leg and side, but his mindspeak was gone and he could speak aloud only haltingly.

Master Ahlee, the *Ahrkeethoheeks'* physician, was candid with the lady-wives of his patient. "At all costs, your husband must remain free from any strain or tension, mental or physical, else he be struck by another paralysis and death certainly ensue. As he is now, it is probable that he never will walk again, and his life hangs by a thread. Naturally, I will stay with him so long as his danger remains grave."

Bili had been two weeks in the duchy, ere he was allowed to see his father for even a few minutes. Dutifully—for the old *Thoheeks'* rank alone deserved deference—the young man knelt by the couch and took his sire's soft, pudgy hand between his own hard ones, speaking in the hushed tones one uses to the gravely ill. "My Lord-Father, can you hear me?"

Both the stricken man's lids twitched, but only the left one opened. Mumbling broken phrases from the left side of his mouth, he asked, "Who is . . . ? Mahrnee? Who is . . . man?"

Mother Mahrnee knelt beside Bili where Hwahruhn could see her, while Mother Behrnees gently opened the lid of his right eye. Placing her firm, freckled arm on the son's shoulders, Mahrnee said, "This is Bili, Hwahruhn. This is your oldest son, husband mine. Do you not remember Bili?"

After kissing his hand, Bili laid it back on the coverlet, saying stiffly, formally, "My Lord Father, I grieve to see you ill." Then he bowed his head, indicating homage, the morning sunlight glinting from his freshly shaven scalp.

Featherlight, trembling fingers brushed his head, then wandered down over cheeks callused by his helmet's face-guards. Finding his scarred chin, they tugged weakly and Bili raised his face.

"Bili . . . ?" His father mumbled chokedly. "Bili, my . . . poor little lad . . . what have . . . they done . . . to you?" Then his brimming black eyes spilled over and tears coursed down his pale cheeks.

The whiterobed physician signed them to leave the

room, and Bili was much relieved to do so. For tutored as he had been, he considered open display of emotion unmanly and was acutely embarrassed by and for his father.

Afterward, the three sat about the winetable in the sisters' sitting room. Mother Behrnees laid her slender fingers on Bili's arm. "Son, do not judge your father by the standards of Harzburk, for the court of cousin Gilbuht is far from Morguhn in many ways. Here, life is different, slower and softer, like the speech. Though I doubt me Hwahruhn has lifted a sword in fifteen years, still is he worthy of your love and respect. For judged by the standards of *his* realm, he is no less manly than are you.

"Your father's Kindred love and respect him, feel him to be good and just and merciful. Until he is more fully recovered of his illness, if ever he is, you will necessarily rule here in his stead. You could do far worse than to emulate those qualities his people so admire."

After blotting watered wine from her pink lips, Mother Mahrnee spoke. "Son, since your return, Behrnees and I have painfully pondered the wisdom of sending you and your brothers—but especially you, the chief and Thoheeks-to-be—for so long a sojourn in the land of our birth. True, those years made of you a full man and warrior. Our hearts were swelled with pride when first we saw you, as you are now so like to the father and brothers we love and remember.

"But as Mother Behrnees just said, this is not Harzburk, and the ways of the Iron Palace are not those of Morguhn Hall. You are certainly aware that King Gilbuht is but the second of his House to rule Harzburk. The grandsire of Gilbuht's grandsire was born heir to only the County of Getzburk, but he died an archduke, having conquered the County of Yorkburk, the Duchy of Tchaimbuhzburk, and the Mark of Tuhseezburk. Archduke Mahrtuhn, Gilbuht's father, secretly financed by the Undying High-Lord Milo, hired enough swords to conquer the Kingdom of Harzburk, slay most of the House of Blawmuh, and settle himself upon the Iron Throne.

"Consequently, Gilbuht's capital is an armed camp and he rules harshly, hating his subjects as fully as they hate him. Had old Mahrtuhn been so stupid as to leave any of the Blawmuhs alive, the rebellions would be more frequent and more stubborn than they presently are.

"So Gilbuht considers his most unwilling subjects cattle and constantly milks them of the monies necessary to pay the troops he must maintain if he is to retain his lands and life."

She paused to sip from her winecup. Then with a rippling of ash-blond tresses, she slowly shook her head. "No, despite his wealth and his power, we would be fools to envy Cousin Gilbuht. Nor would we two trade places with him."

Mother Behrnees nodded her agreement. The sisters agreed on most things; so many things, in fact, that they might almost have been one mind in two beautiful bodies.

"That is why we are now sorry that we badgered your father into sending you, his heir, to Harzburk. For the Kindred of Morguhn will never tolerate the despotism you have seen practiced, nor do most of your people deserve such ill treatment. Yours are not a recently conquered people, son. Through the Ehleenoee line—and do not ever forget, your father and your uncle, the Tahneest are a full three-quarters Ehleen—your forefathers have ruled these lands from time immemorial, and even the Kindred of Morguhn have occupied their station for over a hundred years.

"Precious few of the Ehleen nobility are of pure blood, and all of the other nobles are related to you; so, too, are many of the common people, to a greater or lesser degree. To your Kindred, noble or common, you will be their hereditary chief, not their overlord.

"The true ruler of the duchy, the actual overlord, is the Duchy Council, and although the Chief is its titular head, his voice is but one of fifteen. You . . ." she began, then queried, "The Council, Bili, the Thirds and the reason for their being, what do you recall of them?"

Closing his dark blue eyes, the young man thought deeply for a moment, then took a deep breath. "The Thirds are equals in Council. The first Third is the Thoheeks Chief, the Tahneest, the Clanbard, and the two wisest of the Kindred; the second Third is five noble Ehleenoee; the last Third is five free citizens, Kindred or Ehleen."

"When was the Council established, Bili?" Mother Mahrnee prodded. "And why? And by whose decree?"

Eyes still closed in concentration, he answered, "When first Karaleenos was conquered by the Confederation, the Undying High-Lord did order that the Kindred on whom lands and cities were conferred were not to rule alone, but rather in partnership with the Karaleenee nobles and their people. In this way were rebellions prevented."

Both women smiled and Mother Behrnees declared, "Very good, Bili, almost word-for-word. You've a good memory, and that is well. The Council's regular Moon-meeting is next week and you must, in the Morguhn's absence, sit for him. Remember all that we shall now tell you, for much hinges upon your conduct at that time, not the least of which is the full acceptance of you by the Thirds.

"Now your full uncle, whose name you bear, has always favored you. So much does the Tahneest love you, that I think should you pull out his beard, rape his wife, and raze his hall, you still could depend upon his immediate acceptance of you as the next chief."

Mother Behrnees ticked off another finger. "Cousin Djeen Morguhn is, as you know, a retired Strahteegos, as well as your father's old commander and comrade when they served as Freefighters in the Middle Kingdoms. You won his acceptance last year, when news reached us of your having slain the Earl of Behreesburk in single combat and thus winning your Bear."

Another finger. "Spiros Morguhn has long despised your father for his sedentary, scholarly ways. Talk warfare and weapons and hunting with him and he soon will be your sworn liegeman."

Her last finger curled downward. "The same holds true for Clansbard Hail Morguhn. So simply be what you are, Bili, and the first Third is yours."

She opened her small fist and again ticked off the first finger. "Of the Ehleenoee nobles, Komees Hari and his brother, Drehkos, are your father's third cousins; further, the Komees's first wife, now deceased, was your father's sister. We think that both men can be counted upon to approve your succession, but to be sure, hmmm . . ." She steepled her fingers and regarded Bili closely. "The way your stallion follows you around, you've obviously not lost your touch with horses, so that could be *the* way. What think you, sister?"

"Yes," agreed Mother Mahrnee, nodding. "The horses of Komees Hari are aptly reputed to be among the best in all the Confederation and he is justly proud of them. Immediately we finish here, ride you over to his hall and introduce yourself—he has not seen you in more than ten years and I doubt he would see the boy you were in the man you are.

"Talk horses and keep your hands off his daughters. Ask to see his herd and to meet his kingstallion. Brag of your warhorse some, then mention your desire to purchase a trained hunter. You'll have a bag of gold; of course, he'll refuse to accept it, but the form must be observed.

"After that, my son, it is up to you and your training and your judgment. If you blunder and choose a bad horse . . ." She made a wry face and shrugged meaningfully. "If Hari approves you, Drehkos will usually follow his lead; it is as simple as that."

"The Vahrohnos Myros of Kehnooryos Deskati will

hate you, no matter what you do or say! He will hate you for three reasons, Bili: primarily, because you bear the Morguhn surname; secondly, because you do not look your Ehleen blood; thirdly, because, although you are a handsome man and will no doubt set his parts to itching, you outrank him and so he can neither buy you nor force you into buggery. Be formally polite to the swine, nothing more. And should he dare to offer you open offense, run your steel through his body a few times, and fear no bloodprice. There would be none to demand one anyway, for he hates all things female and so has never wed, and he has outlived all his relatives.

"Myros and *Vahrohneeskos* Stefahnos, who also sits on the second Third—"

"—are both insane!" interrupted Mother Behrnees. "As is that sly, sleek priest and all the poor, common fools they've beguiled into believing their fantasies! If *you* can believe it, Bili, those two and that Blackrobed ass have all but stirred up a rebellion in this duchy!

"Between the agents of Myros and Stefahnos and the priests of that cursed *Kooreeos,* the heads of many—too many—of the Dirtmen and city commoners have been filled with lovely dreams. Those dreams go something like this: the Kindred's farms and Halls and pasturelands, their womenfolk and horses and cattle and their riches are to be evenly divided between all the poor, deserving Dirtmen and urban ne'er-do-wells, which will bring about no work, no want, and idle luxury for all."

Bili could take no more in silence. "Dung and more dung! Without work, there can be nought *save* want. Idle luxury be damned, most nobles labor far harder than any Dirtman or mechanic or tradesman. Why, were it not for . . ."

Mother Mahrnee raised her hand. "Hold, Bili. You know the truth and I know the truth, Myros and Stefahnos and the *Kooreeos* and his damned priests know it. But their dupes do not. The common folks seldom *see* their betters at work, but only the proceeds of that work, they . . ."

Mother Behrnees clanged her empty cup upon the table. "We waste time, sister, and we've damned little of it to waste. Bili knows that the commoners are misled and stupid to swallow such a tale. He can delve into the matter later if he likes, after the Moonmeeting is done.

"For the last Third, son, suffice it to say that there is but one man on whom you can depend. Feelos Pooleeos is now a merchant, but for twenty years he was a soldier in the High-Lord's army, rising as high as *lohkeeas* ere he was done. His loyalty is only to the Confederation, not to the Kindred or to your father. But because the *Thoheeks* represents the established order, while Myros and his scum represent only chaos and anarchy, he will back us and you."

She stared for a long moment at her remaining four fingers, then grimaced and wiped them forcefully upon her skirt, as if she had touched some foulness.

"The rest are all Myros's creatures. Paulos, Guildmaster of the ironsmiths, is your father's halfbrother—one of your grandsire's multitudinous bastards—and Myros has promised him all to which the misbegotten pig aspires: Morguhn Hall, your father to torture to death, you and your brothers as gelded slaves, my sister and me for concubines and so on.

"*Kooreeos* Skiros would be a bishop and see his superstitions paramount in the duchy. We assume Myros has assured him that such would be the case under his overlordship, so a prating pissant supports a pernicious pervert.

"Nathos Ehvrehos, the goldsmith, has extended so much credit to Myros that he can now do nothing save support him, no matter how wild his schemes.

"Djaimos, who stands for the carters and other lesser types, is both a hopeless romantic and a foaming fanatic. He speaks nothing in public save Old Ehleeneekos, goes about in clothing no sane man has worn in a hundred years, and comes near to starving his poor family because he refuses to do business with any of the Kindred or those who do business with them."

As Mother Mahrnee refilled her winecup, Bili asked, "But, My Lady Mothers, you have given me the names of but four of the second Third. Should there not be another?"

"Why, how careless of me." Mother Behrnees slapped palm to forehead, with laughter in her eyes. "How *could* I have forgotten Andee?" After a sly grin at her sister, she addressed herself to Bili.

"Properly, he is *Vahrohnos* Ahndros of Theftehrospolis and he is a Kath'ahrohs, pure Ehleen. Though Ehleen by blood, he identifies with the Kindred and prefers the Mehreekuhn name 'Andee.' Then for ten years he was an officer in the Army of the Confederation. Rising from sublieutenant to company captain in just under eight years, he was chosen for a year of special training at the Staff College in Kehnooryos Atheenahs, after which he served a year on the military staff of the High-Lord, himself. He returned last year just in time to thwart a move by Myros and his clique to legally swindle him out of his patrimony in favor of Andee's cousin, Hahrteeos Toorkos. All this would tend to place him in our camp. But there is another and a better reason we may be certain of his support."

She smiled and directed a devilish glance at her sister. "Andee swoons for love of Mother Mahrnee, Bili! He crowds the roads with hordes of messengers and writes reams of incredibly bad poetry, while the cellars of our hall bulge with his gifts of wines and cordials and spiced meats and sugared fruits. Did my sister respond to calf-eyes and passionate words, their lovesweat would long since have mingled."

Mother Mahrnee laughed. "And do you know it has not already, sister mine?"

The woman's eyes met briefly, then the laughter of Mother Behrnees trilled in harmony with Mother Mahrnee's.

"And so, Bili," Mother Mahrnee said at length, "you know that you may be sure of Andee. He *is* a fine man and closer to your age than any of the others, and I'm . . . well, please tell him that I think of him . . . often."

CHAPTER II

Though not so large as Morguhn Hall, Horse Hall was constructed along the same lines, a mode of building which had originated a hundred years before, when raids by western barbarians were still commonplace. Entering a heavy, iron-studded gate, Bili rode through a dark and narrow passage into a paved courtyard, where a central fountain plashed into a circular stone trough, and a nannygoat and her halfgrown kid drank.

A bowing, smiling servant approached as Bili dismounted, and led Mahvros into the long, two-story building which, pierced by the entry passage, made up the entire front of the hall complex. This building's outer wall was thick and windowless, save for narrow bowman's slits on the upper level. Standing twenty feet from ground to flattopped roof, with square towers rising an additional fifteen feet at each corner and in the center, the front and sides were surmounted by four-foot stone merlons alternating with two-foot-wide crenels.

The walls which connected this structure to the main building were some two feet thick and about fifteen feet high. The walls were also crenellated; a firestep, five feet wide and twelve feet up, ran their length and covered steps connected it with the rooftop fortifications at either end. The colonnades formed by the walks and their supporting columns were the scene of a bustle of activity. An ironsmith and his helpers industriously clanged away near the door through which Mahvros had been led. Opposite him, servant women laughed and chattered, while washing clothing in immense wooden tubs of steaming water. Beyond the women, a gnomelike old man, with a long needle and a leather palmguard, stitched decorations to a dress saddle and half-listened to a travelling bard, who was devoting equal concentration to the tuning of his instrument and to the recitation of lewd stories which he had to almost shout. Nearer to the manor, a man who looked fat enough to be a cook lounged in a cellar doorway supervising a trio of nearnaked boys, who were splitting firewood with a rhythmic chunk-chunking of axes.

At the foot of the wide stairway which led to the main doors, Bili was met by a pudgy, handwringingly servile, bowing man whose black hair and eyes and olive countenance attested him either pure Ehleen or close to it. The upper servant—for such his dress proclaimed him to be—straightened from his last and deepest bow and said, "Greet the Sacred Sun, my master. Wind has borne you well and truly. I am called Hofos and have the honor to be majordomo of the Hall of the Illustrious *Komees* Hari of Daiviz. Whom shall Hofos announce to his master, noble sir?"

Bili said stiffly, "Before I see your master, I would like to wash my face. Also please send someone to dust my clothing. You may announce Bili, eldest son of *Thoheeks* Hwahruhn, Morguhn of Morguhn."

At that, Hofos bowed so far that Bili was sure the man's forehead must soon bump against the flagstones. "Oh, Master of my master, Hofos is humiliated that he failed to recognize the redoubtable *Thoheeks'* son. Hofos begs, he pleads, he most humbly beseeches forgiveness, he . . ."

Bili waved a hand impatiently. He had run into this kind of servant before, and knew Hofos for what he certainly was—dishonest, unscrupulous, and backbiting to his betters, a vicious petty tyrant to his inferiors. Such a servant would never remain long in his employ, he had often vowed, for their unrelenting self-abasement usually concealed an unrelenting hatred of their betters.

"Dammit, man, how could you recognize me, since I've been in Harzburk for ten years? I'll forgive you. Sun and Wind, I'll forgive you nearly anything, if you'll just get on with it!"

Hofos bowed Bili into the hall's foyer and conducted him to a sumptuously appointed bathingroom, where the majordomo issued a barrage of supercilious orders to a trio of bath servants, then backed out, bowing, and scurried off.

Shortly, the carven orkheads above the sunken tub commenced to spout. When the tub was filled and Bili had been expertly divested of swordbelt, boots, and clothing, the two girls and the man saw him safely into the steaming water. While he floated on his back, relaxing in the herbscented bathwater, the servingman departed with Bili's boots and belt and weapons, while the older girl left with his clothing.

After a few minutes, the younger serving girl shed her sandals and her single garment and joined him in the tub. While she laved him from head to foot, he smilingly recalled the first time he had been so attended since his return two weeks agone.

In the northern lands, no more than one full bath per week was the norm among the nobility, though one usually sponged the dust from face and hands after a ride. If anyone at all attended a nobleman's ablutions, it would certainly be a manservant or arming-lad. So when he had first commenced a bath at Morguhn Hall and a pretty, sloe-eyed bathgirl, nude and smiling, had slipped into the water with him, he had reacted as would any Middle Kingdoms noble.

Since that time, Eeoonees had warmed his couch on a dozen nights, and his frequent conversations with her had elicited a plethora of forgotten or half-recalled facts about the distinctly different commoner-noble relationship in the Confederation. Among these nuggets of information was the fact that normally bathgirls were just what their title implied, not concubines.

By the time *Komees* Hari's bathgirl had finished drying his body, the other two attendants had returned with his well-brushed clothing, gleaming leather gear, and freshly polished brass fittings. A cursory glance into his belt purse assured him that the seal on the bag of gold remained unbroken, whereupon he pressed a silver half-thrahkmeh upon each of the three servants—which was far too much, as he knew, but these were the smallest coins his mothers had provided him.

At the doorway of the hall's main room, Hofos stood to one side and bellowed, "Sun and Wind are kind. Now comes the Illustrious Bili, eldest son of our exalted lord, Hwahruhn, *Thoheeks* and Morguhn of Morguhn!"

Near the center of the high-ceilinged chamber, beyond the circular firepit, an elderly and plainly garbed man slouched against the high table. But, when Bili entered, the old man left his place and strode to meet him with a slightly rolling pace which bespoke the fact that much of his life must have been spent ahorse. Bili assumed that this was *Komees* Hari.

The old nobleman's hair was yellow white, his face was lined, and liver spots blotched his big, square hands and thick forearms; otherwise, he bore his fifty-six years admirably. For he was not stooped, though at five-and-a-half feet he was some six inches shorter than Bili, and his brown eyes glittered with intelligence. His grip on his visitor's hand was firm—until Bili actually succeeded to the duchy, he and the *Komees* were equals in rank—and his friendly voice was deep and rolling.

"It's as well that Hofos announced you, Bili, for I'd never have known you otherwise. You are most welcome in my hall. But . . . how fares Hwahruhn, lad?"

Bili shook his head and repeated all that his mothers had been told by Master Ahlee.

His host sighed. "Sacred Sun grant that when I go to Wind, it be a quick death, for if I could not ride among my herds . . . But it may not be so hard on Hwahruhn, for he has done little save read for near twenty years." He sighed again, then draped a long arm about Bili's shoulders.

Smiling, he said, "Come to my office, lad, there's someone I'd like you to meet.

No introduction was needed to recognize the waiting stranger's kinship to the *Komees*. Except for fewer lines in the face, black eyes and black hair shot with grey, he might have been Lord Hari's twin. Nor would Bili have been hardput to name the man's profession, for the calluses on his bluish cheeks and the bridge of his big nose, as well as the permanent dent across the forehead, could only have been caused by a helmet. White against the browned skin, cicatrices of old wounds crosshatched each other on every visible part of his burly body. As he came toward them, he favored his right leg, the thigh of which showed, below his short leather trousers, the purple pink puckering of a still healing injury.

His handgrip was as firm as that of the *Komees* and he precluded a formal introduction by announcing, "Now, it's a real pleasure to meet you, young sir. I am Vaskos Daiviz, natural son of the *Komees*. Despite the wastage of much of my life in dissipation and varied misconduct, my father still allows me his name." His disarming grin showed big, yellow teeth.

Komees Hari chuckled, but when he spoke a fierce pride suffused his voice. "I can think of no living man, Bili, who would not be honored to name Vaskos here his son! When he was fifteen, he enlisted as a spearman in the Army of the Confederation. Now he is a *Keeleechstos* and a weapons master, as well. To attest to his skill and valor, he holds the Order of the Golden Cat! And, when he returns to Kehnooryos Atheenahs from this convalescent leave, he is to be appointed a Substrahteegos. Could any man own a finer son?"

Blushing and fidgeting with embarrassment, the general-to-be gazed at the floortiles. Then, clearing his throat, he changed the subject before more could be said. "My father's wine is superb, sir. But he must talk forever, ere he offers it. My wind is not so long and very little speech tends to dry my throat."

Bili found that the wine was indeed superb. When, after the ritual of mutual healths and toasts to the High-Lord and The Morguhn, the cups were refilled, *Komees* Hari apologized for the absence of his wife and daughters, chuckling ruefully.

"Your arrival, Bili, has set my girls all aflutter—especially Eeyohahnah and Mehleesah, who are at or near marriageable age . . . though where I'll get the gold to dower two more daughters is in the lap of Sacred Sun!"

He shook his white head. "I suppose that peace is wonderful for many of our Confederation, but it spells hard times for a man whose livelihood is the breeding of war-horses, what with high taxes and a profusion of daughters to be adequately dowered.

"You see, lad, Vaskos is my only son. None of my wives' male infants lived more than a couple of weeks; and, can I secure Council's approval, he'll be my heir. How could any Council refuse to grant legitimacy to a Strahteegos of our Confederation? Although after I've provided dots for Eeyohahnah and Mehleesah and little Behtee, my title, my sword, and my ledgerbooks are about all I'll probably be able to leave him.

"I vow, Bili, were it not for a few good and faithful customers in the Middle Kingdoms and the Black Kingdoms, my family and I would be starving and in rags!"

Bili was nobody's fool. His mission here was to win the support of the aging *Komees*. What better way than to offer his help in furtherance of the old nobleman's ambition for his bastard? It was certain to be more effective than the simple choice and purchase of a horse he really did not need.

Besides, he had liked the officer and he genuinely admired him and his accomplishments. A *Keeleechstos,* leader of three thousand men—in the Middle Kingdom, his rank would be colonel—just might have attained to that rank through the skillful greasing of selected palms. But in the Army of the Confederation it was well known that Strahteegoee were chosen strictly upon the grounds of ability; too, there was that Golden Cat. While thousands of Red Cats and hundreds of Silver Cats had been awarded during the century since the establishment of the orders, less than fivescore men, all told, had ever won the right to a golden one, of any class.

"Lord Hari," he began.

"Now stop that, Bili!" admonished his host. "You've clearly been too long away from home, among those stiffnecked northerners. We of the Kindred call each other by name, reserving formality for superiors, strangers, and known enemies. I'm Hari and my son is Vaskos."

"All right, Hari," Bili started over. "I'll be candid. I want something of you, and you want something of Council. Pledge me support in my aims, and I, in turn, will pledge you my support and my best efforts at gaining the support of others in attaining your aspiration for Vaskos."

And so, we sing a proud song,
Of Pitzburk, where the siege was long,
Of Pitzburk, where our rivers ran with blood.

The last note died. Klairuhnz, the traveling bard, lowered his instrument and slowly bowed.

Bili's fingers sought his purse and selected a silver thrahkmeh. The singer deserved it, for he had certainly rendered an excellent performance, what with ancient tellingsongs of the exploits of Morguhn and Daiviz chiefs and clansmen now hundreds of years dead; a couple of Ehleen loveballads which had even brought a few brief smiles to the jowly, perpetually frowning face of the Lady Hehrah, Lord Hari's short, immensely fat wife; a Freefighter song, much laundered, which nonetheless had every man in the room roaring, since the words replacing the bawdy ones did not rhyme, making the original lyrics easy to guess; and ending with the famous *Song of Pride*, a venerable favorite in the Middle Kingdoms, though not so well known this far south.

Allowing his host and Vaskos to throw their coins first, Bili then tossed his thrahkmeh. The bard caught the three silver pieces in flight, juggled them for a few moments, then lined them on his open left palm. Closing that hand, he made a gesture or two above it with his right hand and, when he reopened the left, all three coins were gone.

The two youngest of Lord Hari's three daughters *oohed* and *ahhed* their amazement, but the older, Eeyohahnah, never changed expression, since she did not see the sleight-of-hand. Her dark, brooding, slightly slanted eyes had never left Bili since first they were introduced; they had followed his every movement or gesture throughout the dinner. However, on each of the several occasions he had attempted to meet her stare, she had looked down with a show of modesty and the barest flicker of a sly smile. Her activities were beginning to irk Bili, but it would be undignified and most impolitic to allow his discomfiture to become noticeable.

Bili was far from a novice in the ways of women. Since first his voice had deepened and his shoulders commenced to broaden, women and girls had made no secret of the fact that they found him handsome to look upon. He had been but fourteen when he had pleasurably spent his virginity within the young widow of the Earl of Dawfuhnburk, then living at King Gilbuht's court. After her, he had tumbled countless serving girls and had paid court to and bedded other idle noblewomen.

He had been introduced to rapine at the ghastly intaking of Indersburk and again, more recently, had renewed his acquaintance when Behreesburk fell. But this girl, this Eeyohahnah, was no spoil of war, to be stripped and enjoyed at his leisure. Nor was she a lustful servingwench or a promiscuous northern grasswidow, free to take the bedpartner of her choice.

That the ravenhaired girl was nubile was more than apparent, even through the folds of her old-fashioned Ehleen himation, especially since she had, seemingly by accident, pulled the garment tight over her firmly swelling breasts. But the very fact that the girls and their mother were all dressed so anachronistically attested that Eeyohahnah had been reared in the Ehleen manner, and Bili knew that Ehleenoee nobles placed an absurdly high value on virgin brides. All rational men agreed that the crucified god of the Ehleenoee alone knew why they clove to so stupid a custom.

So it angered Bili that she would thus flaunt herself and taunt him with what she knew he could not take the pleasure of without so deeply offending Lord Hari that he would probably end up having to kill the old man in a death match . . . either that or marry the brazen chit. And, it came to him, maybe *that* was at the core of the matter. She knew that he would be *Thoheeks* sooner or later, and fancied herself a fair candidate for *Thoheekeesa* of Morguhn.

Well, she was no such thing! When *Thoheeks* Bili wed, he had no intention of taking an unproven heifer, not for his senior wife anyway. The woman he would take for that would have proven couchskills and would also have a proven ability to conceive.

But Lord Hari was speaking, commanding, "A chair and wine for Bard Klairuhnz." Then, to the bard, "You are, I am informed, lately come from the Southern

Duchies. Tell us the news, when you have had of the wine."

The blackhaired singer sat on the chair and carefully lowered his harp to the floor, then accepted the mug of wine. His Adam's apple bobbed as he downed half the mug. Leaning back, he smiled contentedly as the warmth the spirit spread through his vitals.

"Another of the ancient horseclans," he began, "has crossed the southern mountains and has been recognized as True Kindred by *Ahrkeethoheeks* Djaimz. The clan is that of Sanderz and they live according to the tenets of the *Couplets of the Law*. Even now, their chief, Hwahltuh by name, journeys to Kehnooryos Atheenahs to pledge his Kindred Oath to the High-Lord."

"Do *you* believe them truly of our Kindred, Bard Klairuhnz?" inquired the *Komees*. "In times past, I hear, there have been bands of nomads who so claimed, in order to be granted lands . . ."

The bard nodded vigorously. "Oh, these are genuine Kindred, Lord *Komees*, I've no doubt of that. Lord Djaimz had me seek out the Sanderz bard, and he knows the Law—*all* of the Law! Also, he sung me the entire *Song of Sanderz*, which took most of a day. They are most certainly of the *Children of Ehlai*, the original Kindred. Their Old Mehreekuhn is the purest I have heard in years, and those who can tell say that almost all of the Sanderz can mindspeak."

This last was a telling point. Mindspeak—telepathic ability—was once an ages-old inherent talent of eighty percent of the Kindred. On the Plains which the Kindred had roamed for hundreds of years, before forty-odd of the clans had first invaded the Ehleen lands, mindspeak talents had constituted a definite survival factor, as well as the only way of communicating with Prairie Cat and horse. Even with the blood of those original forty-odd clans much thinned by generations of intermarriage with other peoples, many of the modern Kindred still possessed mindspeak, to a greater or lesser degree. Bili had it, as did both the *Komees* and Vaskos, and so—though he was damned careful of who knew—did Bard Klairuhnz.

"The sea—" the bard continued his news, the transmission of which between farflung duchies was one of the most valuable and welcome functions of the traveling bards "—still is rising along the coasts and more farmland is being lost each year, as the salt fens widen. Sea creatures venture ever farther up the rivers as well, and the talk in the Southern Duchies has been of the huge white shark—a full dozen meters long and far thicker and heavier than most of that ilk, with teeth half as long as a man's finger—slain in the pleasure lake of the *Ahrkeethoheeks*. It overturned three boats and slew or drowned near a score of boatmen and soldiers ere—all its monstrous body abristle with arrows and darts and spears—it was finally driven into shallows and clubbed and axed to death.

"So many of the soldiers and waterpeople swore that the shark fought with the reasoning of a man rather than the mere cunning of a beast that the *Ahrkeethoheeks* had a boatload of Ehleen priests brought down from his capital, giving them leave to conduct their ceremonies for driving demons from the lake and the land. I myself saw some of those rites, and right awesome they were."

"Hogwash!" snorted the *Komees*. "Young Djaimz must be as weakbrained as was his father, to put any faith in Ehleen superstitions. If he really wanted to be sure that that lake was cleared, he should have rented or borrowed some Orks from the Lord of the Sea Isles. No known waterbeast is the match of a few of those thirtyfooters!

"And it is a pure mystery to me, Bard Klairuhnz, why God-Milo failed to slay every one of those pimps in priests' clothing, those holy slavers, on whom he could lay hands a hundred years agone! All the bastards, from the lowest *Eeyehrefsee* to the *Ahrkeeyehpeeskohpohs* himself, are powerhungry and athirst for Kindred blood . . . or

Kindred gold, whichever seems easiest to lay their scaly hands to.

"Why, that thrice-accursed *Kooreeos* Skiros of Morguhnpolis had the nerve to come to me, no more than a year agone, and demand—mind you, Kinsmen, not ask, but *demand*—one of my daughters for a 'bride' for his god, complete with a dowry which was to be paid to him."

"So what answer did you give the holy man, Father?" asked Vaskos, grinning hugely. He had obviously heard the tale before, and enjoyed it.

A harsh, humorless laugh came from the *Komees*. "I told him that since I did not follow or honor his stupidities, he had no claim on me or mine. That it has been known for a hundred years that he and his kind are whoremongers and slavers and that I would slay every one of my daughters, ere I consigned them to his 'care.' And I warned him against returning to Horse Hall, since the next time he trespassed under my roof, I'd make him 'hole-y,' in truth!"

He turned his face to Bili. "Lad, I'm sorry to have to criticize your father, but over the years he has been far too lax in his handling of potentially dangerous malcontents in this duchy. Myros of Kehnooryos Deskati, for instance, should've been flogged the length of these lands and hanged ten years ago. Your uncle, the Tahneest, favored it, as did *Komees* Djeen and I and Clanbard Hail and even your mothers; but *Thoheeks* Hwahruhn would list to none of us, and now his duchy, and all of us with it, sits in the pan of a cocked catapult!

"Mark my words, Bili, bad days are coming to these lands. Myros's agitation was bad enough, but since this arrogant *Kooreeos* arrived four years ago, the petty Ehleenoee nobles and most of the commoners—city and rural—are become secretive and surly. I fear that terrible things are afoot."

"Aye," agreed Klairuhnz. "Ever do the squarebeards

foment unrest amongst their followers. And no matter how much freedom is given them, they demand more and ever more. Why, in Gafnee . . ."

Komees Hari's bony knuckles glowed white against the sunbrowned skin of his clenched hands and his voice grated. "Yes, Kinsman, we heard even here; and my son, Vaskos, has told me still more. A nasty business. Sacred Sun grant that our troubles never get so far!"

"Heard what, Bard Klairuhnz?" asked Bili impulsively, noticing neither the rage on the face of his hostess, nor the grim set of his host's features.

So abruptly and violently did *Komeesa* Hehrah arise that her chair went crashing over. In an icy voice and clipped phrases, she said, "My lords, the hour is late. Too, I have heard quite enough slander of dedicated, selfless clergymen, I beg leave to retire. Eeyohahnah, Mehleesah, Behtee . . . come!"

Spinning, she waddled to and through the doorway, trailed by her daughters and servingwomen, bidding a goodnight to no one.

"I take it, Lord *Komees*," the Bard drily remarked, "that My Lady cleaves to the Ehleen religion."

Lord Hari made a rude noise, disgust and anger on his face. Grasping an ewer, he filled his mug to the brim, drank it all down, then slammed the empty mug onto the table with enough force to set dishes and cutlery to dancing. After taking several deep breaths, he spoke in a well-controlled voice, his first words directed to Bili.

"I apologize for My Lady's atrocious conduct, Kinsman."

Bili squirmed in his chair. "My Lord, perhaps if I had not asked the question of Bard Klairuhnz . . . ?"

"No, Bili," the old lord sighed. "It was coming, and I well knew it. My Lady ever goes out of her way to offer offense to any Kindred I entertain, only showing her good side around folk of her own ilk. In the last few years, she's become almost unbearable."

"But, why . . . ?" Bili began.

Looking as if he needed to spit, *Komees* Hari answered before Bili finished asking. "Because among her innumerable other failings, my cursed wife slavishly bides by every one of the old Ehleen superstitions and practices, including some of the vilest of them. Oh, warm and loving *Sun!*" He beat one big fist against his wiry thigh, soul-deep pain shining from his eyes.

"*Why*, oh, why was not my father more careful? Had he but known how rotten was My Lady's blood with all the cursed, shameful Ehleen practices, this day would see me wed to her I truly loved, Vasko's dear mother, not to that perverted, demonridden sow, Hehrah!

"Bili, all else aside, I know why you came. Rather, why you were *sent* to my hall, today. Your dear mothers are wise and were thinking straight and properly, but it was not really necessary, for your House has ever had my support in Council and *you* will always have it. I can speak for my brother, Drehkos as well, I believe. As for . . ."

But then Hofos, the majordomo, advanced up the hall, bowing and wringing his hands, to announce the arrival of noble guests.

CHAPTER III

Shortly, Bili, Vaskos, and Klairuhnz were seated with wine, cheese, fruit, and pipes in the *Komees*'s study-cum-armory, awaiting the arrivals of Lord Hari and his guests. Once the winecups were filled and the Bard and Vaskos had their pipes going well, Bili addressed Klairuhnz.

"All right, Kinsmen, what in hell happened in the lands of *Komees* Gafnee that caused Lady Hehrah to take such umbrage at the mere mention of it?"

"Well-l-l . . ." drawled Klairuhnz, with an inquiring glance at Vaskos.

The officer chuckled. "You may speak freely, Bard. I hold to Sun and Wind, like my father. I may *look* like an Ehleen, but my heart is that of a Horseclansman. Further, having served the Confederation for so many years, I can spare scant sympathy for those who would see its dissolution. I know of the Gafnee business, of course, for I've talked with officers whose units helped to mop up the mess. Bili's a right to know, for it would appear that matters are building up to a similar problem here, unless a certain *Vahrohnos*—you two may be unaware of the fact that the same bastard was cashiered from our army!—and a passel of bloodthirsty priests are right speedily executed or banished."

The Bard nodded brusquely, drained off his mug, then asked, "My Lord Bili, how much know do you of the Ehleen priests and their sect?"

Bili shrugged. "Damned little, I'm afraid. None of our

hall practice it, none that I know of anyway. And it is unheard of in the Middle Kingdoms—the sword being worshiped there, though a few women do hold to the Blue Lady."

Klairuhnz puffed at his pipe and eyed his audience through a cloud of bluish smoke. "The sect is old, Bili, ancient really. It's at least as old as the first Ehleen kingdoms—say, seven hundred years. But the Ehleenoee apparently brought it and its priests with them when they crossed the Great Sea and invaded these lands, and I have talked with Ehleen scholars who held that their religion was two thousand years old at the time of the War of the Gods. And men say that that calamity occurred nearly twelve hundred years ago! Of course, many doubt that contention, but who can say truly, after so much time?

"Ere the Kindred came, the Ehleen sect had been slowly dying for a hundred or more years, and what few followers it retained were mostly lower or middleclass—peasants, mechanics, tradesmen, small merchants, and suchlike. Most of the Ehleen nobility had adopted some odd and rather sinister cults—the worship of monstrous animals, fish, and serpents, to whom they frequently sacrificed living humans. But as more of the Ehleenoee became dispossessed of their lands and cities, during the Wars of Confederation and the sporadic rebellions, the *Eeyehrefsee* advertised themselves and their religion as a rally point for those of their race, and many of the nobles went back to what they called the Ancient Faith.

"Now the Horseclansmen were ever tolerant of the harmless beliefs of other peoples. Once the High-Lord had exposed the misdeeds of the *Eeyehrefsee* of Kehnooryos Ehlahs—which ranged from shady business practices and smuggling to whoremongering and slaving—broken their power, stripped them of most of their ill-gotten profits, and smashed their financial empire, they were allowed to practice their rites almost unmolested.

"But the last twenty years have seen rapid and very

ominous changes in the sect. Certain of the darker practices of the monster cults have crept into the rites of the Ancient Faith, and here and there a priest or a *Kooreeos* has taken it into his head to foment disorder and even open, armed rebellion—on the order of the *Djeehahd* or 'Holy War' in which certain of the Black Kingdoms sometimes engage.

"Mostly, such insanities have been scotched before they got much out of hand. Alert Kindred nobles who weren't afraid to shed a little blood for the good of all their peoples simply seized the squarebeards and their lay ringleaders, publicly tried them, publicly executed them, and then imported new *Eeyehrefsee* who had more interest in keeping their heads attached to their bodies.

"But *Komees* Peetuh, who was Regent of Gafnee for a *Thoheeks*-son who was not yet of age, lived and died a very foolish man." Then the Bard went on to describe the highlights of the Gafnee Horror—a loathsome tale of a rabble risen at the urgings of priests and led by noble Ehleen malcontents; of halls besieged, overrun, looted, then burned; of Kindred men tortured to death; of Kindred ladies dying horribly beneath the lusts of hundreds of attackers; of the blood-drenched sacrifices of Kindred children and babes to the dark god of the gory-pawed Ehleen priests.

It was Klairuhnz's profession to spin good tales and he was a past master at his art. The pictures he spoke were real—terribly real. Both Bili and Vaskos could see the surging, bloodthirsty mobs and hear their savage roarings, could hear the clash of arms and the crackling of the fires and the screams of the wounded or tormented or dying, could smell the smoke of burning halls and the stink of burning flesh in the Bard's words.

The priests had been shrewd in the timing of their rising, choosing the beginning of what promised to be a bad winter, when communications between principalities would be sketchy at best. And what few travelers did enter the Duchy of Gafnee never left it; the sinister *Eeyehrefsee* saw to that. When, with the late arrival of spring, it came time for the New Year Council, all the nobles of the Archduchy were surprised at the absence of *Komees* Peetuh, who had ere been one of the first arrivals at Lohfospolis.

Ahrkeethoheeks Eevahnos delayed the Council for a couple of days and sent an officer of his guard to see what might be detaining his old friend. When that officer failed to return, another officer was sent, along with a half troop of horseguards. None of those men ever came back either, but a couple of wounded troophorses stumbled in. The saddle of one was covered in crusted blood, and a mind-speaker got from both animals a story of deceit and butchery.

"At that juncture," Klairuhnz continued, "Lord Eevahnos had the hillfires lit and called up the levy. With the spearlevymen and the Kindred cavalry and the Freefighters of his guard, he sealed the borders of Gafnee and initiated tentative scoutings into it, while his messengers rode north, west, and south.

"It so happened that Strahteegos *Vahrohnos* Fil Kuk of Kukpolis was on the march to the Southern Duchies with three thousand kahtahfrahktoee. He and his two squadrons were encamped near Gastohnya, when one of the *Ahrkeethoheeks*'s gallopers happened that way.

"He at once broke camp. By dawn, he was on Gafnee's northern border, where he picked up a few Kindred cavalry and a troop of Freefighters, then swept down into Gafnee, to the very gates of Gafneepolis. And there they camped until Eevahnos and his ragtag army joined them.

"Now the original city of Gafneepolis was razed by King Zastros's army a hundred years ago, and wasn't rebuilt for about ten years. Having nothing to fear, they thought, those who built its walls made them neither thick nor high and pierced them for double the usual number of gates. Such a position, defended as it was principally by priests, peasants, and tradesmen, had not a chance against the attack of professionals. It fell quickly."

Pausing to take a pull of his mug, Klairuhnz would have taken time to relight his pipe, but Bili could not wait.

"And then?" he urged. "What then, Kinsman?"

Vaskos spoke. "Apply you to your pipe, Bard Klairuhnz. I'll try to finish the tale. True, I was not there, but as I said, I've friends who were.

"Well, Bili, when the *Ahrkeethoheeks* and his nobles became aware of just what had transpired in Gafnee that winter, they commenced to tremble in their boots, as well they should've. First, they scoured all of Gafnee for survivors and found not one living noble Kindred in all the duchy . . . nor did the searchers leave any living person behind them—priest, peasant, or villager, man, woman, or child, those who did not surrender quickly died!"

"Good!" Bili nodded. "That was good work."

Vaskos stared levelly at the young man for a moment, not noticing the odd smile on the Bard's face. "Think you so, Kinsman? Then hear the rest.

"The *Ahrkeethoheeks* had hundreds of people put to savage tortures and got the names of all the lay ringleaders. All who were still living on that list of names, he cast into the town dungeons, along with the priests.

"With all the living Gafneeans completely disarmed and confined, helpless as babes in the city, the *Ahrkeethoheeks* gave the Confederation troops and his own complete freedom of the city for seven days—allowed them to loot and burn and rape and torment and kill to the point of utter satiation. He and his nobles sent wagon after groaning wagon of loot back to Lohfospolis, as well as all the grain and livestock on which they could lay hands!

"It took the pitiful wretches who survived that week of carnage another week to breach their walls to their conquerors' satisfaction, pull down their gates, and dig a long, deep trench just outside the city. Then the *Ahrkeethoheeks* assembled the couple of thousand Gafneeans under guard by all his forces. He had the priests and lay leaders dragged out and stripped naked, even the women!"

"Women?" Bili looked bewildered.

"Yes, Bili," nodded Vaskos. "Some of the lay leaders were women. And right horribly were they treated.

"The priests and the male leaders were gelded, then pitch was poured on their wounds. That barbarity done with, the *Ahrkeethoheeks* set his guardsmen to striking the heads from every man, woman, and child of Gafnee, forcing the priests and leaders who had not died of their maltreatment to watch the butchery."

"All of the female leaders naturally died of their sufferings, but some score of the priests and male leaders lived. They were set on the road, still naked and with their lips stitched shut, loaded with a manweight of manacles and chains, in two wagons and heavily guarded. Less than half lived to reach Kehnooryos Atheenahs!"

Failing to note the disgust and horror on Vaskos's swarthy face, Bili commented casually, "Sewed their lips shut, did he? Well, that's one march Lord Eevahnos has stolen on King Gilbuht. It was a good idea too, keep the bastards from spreading their poison along the way or from plotting amongst themselves. But, tell me, Kinsman, how did the rebel swine eat and drink?"

In lieu of answer, Vaskos asked in a tight voice, "Have you no feeling, then? That civilized men could do such things in the name of justice and our Confederation sickens me! To so mistreat conquered enemies . . ."

"Conquered rebels," corrected Bili. "There is a considerable difference, you know. That, Kinsman, is the only way to handle the kind of rebellion you and Klairuhnz have described. You must put it down so hard and so thoroughly that no commoner or priest or noble will ever forget the fate of a rebel. I, for one, would like to make the acquaintance of this Lord Eevahnos. He sounds like a wise and most astute man. Why, King Gilbuht himself could not have done a better job!"

"But to slay women and children . . . even babes . . ." Vaskos began.

"Nits make lice, Kinsman!" Bili shrugged.

Vaskos's visage darkened perceptibly, and he straightened in his chair. "I have been a soldier for above thirty years, and while I've had to put my steel into a few barbarian women, I've yet to slay a child. Nor will I, ever!"

Bili raised his right hand, palm to Vaskos in the ancient gesture of peace. "Kinsman, I but requested a tale, not an argument. There is no need for your anger. But ere I see it grow, I shall take my leave." Arising, he smoothed his suede gambeson and started to buckle the tops of his jackboots.

"Now, hold!" snapped Klairuhnz, unmistakeable authority in his voice. "You, Kinsman Bili, sit down! You, Kinsman *Keeleechstos* Vaskos, act your age and your rank! The Confederation has scant need of hotheaded Strahteegoee!"

With Bili once more in his chair and Vaskos silent, the Bard leaned forward and continued, slowly and forcefully, his black eyes hard. "None of us here is as innocent as you would have us believe you to be, Kinsman Vaskos. *I* have slain children, Kinsman Bili has slain children, and so too have *you*! Think you, how many men have died under your steel, do you suppose? In above thirty years soldiering, the number must be large, considering all the small wars and skirmishings against the mountainfolk. So how many children starved to death, because you had slain their fathers?"

Vaskos shifted in his chair, looking down at his big hands, and mumbled, "But that's not the same."

The Bard nodded vehemently. "Correct. Correct, *Keeleechstros* Vaskos, it is not the same at all. For the sword offers a clean, quick death, while the death of hunger is long and slow, torturous and incredibly horrible, with the body ravenously feeding upon its own flesh and blood and muscle. Many of those children, Vaskos, would have welcomed the cold, sharp kiss of your sword . . . aye, and blessed you for your mercy!"

And suddenly Bili was there, was one of them! One of the horde of shadowy, emaciated little starvelings—all sunken, hungerbright eyes and swollen abdomens, arms and legs fleshless and reedthin, hands like tiny claws and faces like skincovered skulls, suppurating, dripping sores and teeth dropping from bleeding gums. His hand weakly fumbled for his winemug . . . *anything* to fill his gaping, agonizing emptiness.

Then the nightmare dissolved as suddenly as it had come. "Sorry, Bili," came a mindspeak from Klairuhnz, on a level which Bili had thought he alone possessed, having never before met another who could communicate on it. "That was intended for Vaskos, not for you."

The Bard would then have broken off the mental connection, but Bili held stubbornly to it, demanding, "Who in hell are you, truly? *What* are you? No common mindspeaker could've done what you just did—that I know! And no man, possessing such powers as you have would waste his life and talents as a mere traveling bard. Are you then a sorcerer in disguise?"

"Sorcerers are nonexistent, Bili," came the quick reply. "There are only men and women who use their inherent powers to the detriment or death of others . . . much as you effected the death of Earl Hahnz, or magnified the sound of your warhorses's hooves, so that those brigands thought a troop was charging them."

Bili started, and his right hand clamped onto the hilt of his dirk. "How . . . what do *you* know of . . . ?"

"Only what I was able to glean from your mind, earlier in the dininghall. But fear not, Bili, those secrets are safe. Nor do I fault you, for in a fight to the death, only a fool would refrain from employing every weapon or skill at his disposal."

"Who and what," Bili repeated insistently, "are you?"

"You shall know, in time," was the Bard's curt answer. "You shall know all that you now ask, and much, much more. But for now, drink your wine and allow me to finish Vaskos's education, for I . . . *we* . . . may soon have need of him."

On the mindspeak level, the exchanges had taken bare fractions of seconds. And Vaskos, whose mindspeak talents were marginal at best, was unaware that Bili and Klairuhnz had even conversed.

"Perhaps all that you say is right," he answered the Bard's most recent statement. "But even so, that is but scant justification for the atrocities and wholesale butchery at Gafnee. The rebels could've been dispersed to other places, or even sold overseas. But to coldly slaughter them . . . I, for one, could never . . ."

Slowly, Klairuhnz shook his head. "Vaskos, you have a great capacity for compassion. Used properly, it will aid you in being a better-than-average Strahteegos. Utilized imprudently, allowed to rule rather than serve you, at the wrong time and toward the wrong people, as you are presently doing, it will lead to your downfall, if not your death.

"Vaskos, Vaskos, you are thinking with your huge loving heart, and not with the mind of a talented and experienced soldier, a leader of men. Think, man, *think*!"

Vaskos's forehead furrowed. "What mean you, Bard?"

"All right, look at it this way," Klairuhnz tried another tack. "You have fought the Tcharlztuhnee, I take it?"

Vaskos nodded brusquely. "Aye, our most recent campaign was against those devils."

Klairuhnz went on. "They steep their arrow-, dart-, and spearpoints in a fermented dung. So what do the *eeahtrosee* to such a wound, say to a deep thrust in the leg?"

Vaskos's lips tightened. "They slash the leg to the bone, let the man's own blood wash and cleanse the wound, then they poultice it with pledgets of molded wheaten-bread. But what has such to do with . . . ?"

"All in due time." Klairuhnz cut Vaskos's question off short. "And if the bleeding and the poultices fail, Vaskos, if the toes blacken and the leg purples and starts to stink, what, then, do the *eeahtrosee*?"

Vaskos sighed gustily. "What can they do, if the man is to live? They dose him well with hwiskee or strong cordials, bludgeon him unconscious, then cut off the leg." Absently, he rubbed at his scarred thigh:

"Odd, but I was wounded, just so, by a Tcharlztuhnee spear. But the bleeding and poultices worked, in my case. Very odd, indeed, Kinsman Klairuhnz, that your example should have been a wound so like to mine own."

Bili smiled into his winecup. Considering what he had just learned of the so-called Bard's abilities in delving minds, he did not consider the incident at all odd.

"Just a coincidence," Klairuhnz shrugged, adding, "But that course of treatment is used on a fresh wound, Vaskos. Let us say that the wounded man was pinned under a dead horse, and lay on the field for a day or so, ere he was found by the eeahtrosee. What then?"

"They'd take no chances," stated Vaskos soberly. "They'd have the leg off almost at once."

"Why?" demanded Klairuhnz.

"Sun and Wind, man," Vaskos burst out. "Because if they waited too long, or didn't take the leg at all, the poisons would possibly spread throughout the entire body and kill the man."

Then Klairuhnz said, "Vaskos, the Confederation is a social body. The Gafnee rebellion was a wound to that body, a seriously infected wound. That infection was well commenced, ere Strahteegos Kuk and the *Ahrkeethoheeks* came to treat it. To have dispersed the rebels would have been to insure the infection of other parts of the body, the Confederation. Therefore, like *eeahtrosee,* they excised the infection, removed it cleanly, did everything within their power to halt its spread.

"Yes, Vaskos, the Gafnee executions were an extreme measure and the hearts of many would brand them cruel, but the mind must see it for what it truly was: a necessary expedient, intended to restore the health of the Confederation!"

CHAPTER IV

Komees Djeen Morguhn was tall, even taller than Bili, and spare. He marched rather than walked, striding to the silent beat of a personal drum. His face would have been handsome as Bili's, save for the long scar, which in healing had twisted his upper lip into a perpetual grin, and had taken his left eye as well. He was also missing most of one ear, the last two fingers of his swordhand, and his left hand and wrist, which had been replaced by a shiny brass cap and hook. His scars and his limp were the marks of his former profession. Despite the aches and pains, which increased with every year and were accentuated by damp weather, *Komees* Djeen counted himself very lucky, for precious few career soldiers ever saw their sixtieth year.

He never really felt dressed unless some manner of armor weighted his shoulders. Tonight it was a hiplength jacket of brigandine, cinched about his narrow waist by an Army swordbelt supporting his purse and plain, well-worn dirk. Between the lower hem of the brigandine and the still buckled tops of his jackboots could be seen his sensible, linencanvas breeches.

The short man who followed him went garbed in the simple, five-piece ensemble of the Horseclansman—loose, pullover shirt; wide, big-buckled dirkbelt; and baggy trousers tucked into short, soft boots. His only armament was a broadbladed rancher's knife. Though he could not recall ever having seen him, Bili had no trouble in identifying him as Lord Drehkos, *Komees* Hari's brother, for the two men were like as peas in a pod.

The third man, however, was an utter stranger. He was about Bili's height, and like him his shoulders were wide and thick; his long arms ended in a big, wide hands. But there the similarity ended, for the man was obviously a *Kath'ahrohs* or fullblood Ehleen. His long pomaded hair was blueblack and his skintone, like Vaskos's, was a dark olive, though his finer features made him a far more handsome man.

This stranger was garbed in black, from foot to pate. His delicately grained, glovesoft boots rose to midthigh. Both they and his belt had been buffed until they threw back the lamplight like expanses of onyx. His sleeveless tunic encased him from shoulders to boottops and was wrought of that thick, lustrous velvet for which the Duchy of Klahksburk was justly famous. The sleeves of his silken shirt billowed from shoulder to wrist, where they were drawn tight, and atop his head drooped a soft cap of the Klahksburk, its center and edges adorned with arabesques stitched out in silver wire. The case and hilt of his dress dirk were of black leather, the former edged and studded with silver and the latter wound with silver wire; its pommel consisted of a bright silver ball almost two inches in diameter. Also silver was the massy, flatlink chain which was draped over his shoulders, but the pendant it supported was gold.

While his rich clothing and accessories would not have been considered remarkable in the Middle Kingdoms or even at the court of the Undying High-Lord, within an austerely oldfashioned province such as the Duchy of Morguhn, impractical fripperies were the mark of the fop. Bili had impulsively catalogued the newcomer as such until his eyes lit on what depended from the silver chain.

No man's rank or lineage or lands or fortune ever brought him into the Order of the Cat. Only well-witnessed acts of extreme valor in fierce combat earned even a Ninth Class Red Cat. So this stranger was anything but a fop, for his pendant—brilliant against the black velvet—bore the stalking shape of the Golden Cat, bright emeralds serving as its eyes. It was a Fourth Class Cat and gave notice to all who saw it to honor this man for the mighty champion he was.

Deep in the cellars of Horse Hall, another meeting was in progress. There, a score or so of figures crouched in the musty darkness amid the winetuns and brandy kegs and vats of pickled vegetables. The only light came from a smoky lamp, which rendered faces and forms vague and wraithlike. Although the door to their meetingchamber was well guarded, they kept their voices lowpitched and spoke only in Old Ehleeneekos, the language spoken before the Coming of the Horseclans more than a century before, now almost dead and seldom heard outside Ehleen Church rites.

From the darkness a slightly nasal voice declared, "I say we should kill them all. Here and now, tonight!"

"And I agree." A coldly arrogant voice half-snarled from the other side. "When our time is ripe, the Butter-haired Devils still will be struggling to recover from so great a loss. *Think*, up there sit the heir apparent to the *Thoheeks*, two *Komeesee*, a *Vahrohneeskos*, a City Lord, plus that bard and the Bastard."

"You are both fools!" A dry, authoritarian woman's voice flatly averred. "Oh, I doubt me not that the strangling cord or the unexpected knifethrust are disciplines with which you have much familiarity, but how much do any of you know of the art of the sword? Eh? Ere you had slain the Bastard's man, who sits guard before their door, and battered that thick portal down, your would-be victims would be assuredly warned . . . and the Hall armory is in that room, you know."

"Lady, we too have arms." The nasal first voice insisted stubbornly.

"You most certainly are fools, to talk so," said a new voice, deep and rolling. "And I speak of sure knowledge, being the only trained soldier among you. Your arms are old relics and, despite my best efforts over these last months, few of you have absorbed even the bare bones of the use of those arms.

"Most of those men up there are *professional* soldiers, or they were. The one who is not was still reared a Kindred nobleman, which means reared to the sword. Of that bard, I know naught, save that his horse be war-trained and his harness includes a well-balanced and well-kept saber, which I doubt he carries as a toothpick. Attempt the idiocy of which you prate and the most of you will die tonight. And your well-hacked corpses will be of no use to the Church or to our oppressed people."

"Phah! Don't listen to the coward," hissed the arrogant second voice. "*He* is not our leader!"

"The last man who named me coward," the deep voice rolled menacingly, "died with his guts curled around his legs!"

"Enough!" snapped the woman. "Would you men serve the very cause of the Oppressors? Remember your oaths and the sacredness of our crusade."

"I do remember my oath, Lady," the soldier softly boomed. "It is the only reason I have not removed the heads from some of these yapping curs long since!" Then, speaking to the others in the room, "No, I am not your leader, thank God. But your leader did appoint me your advisor. And my advice is this: Wait. Wait for the opportunity to kill without being killed."

The nasal voice suggested, "Why don't we just poison the roomful? They are sure to call for more wine, ere the night's out."

"We dare not," answered the woman, quickly. "One of them is secretly one of us."

"Tell me which he is." Another female voice. "Lady, I could serve them, and sign him not to drink . . ."

But the commanding female advised, "No. We do not know who he is, and even if we did, it were too dangerous to make Sacred Signs before so many."

"Besides," rumbled the advisor. "How would you know which signs still are secret? How would anyone know . . . since Gafnee?"

Mere mention of the terrible calamity brought the expected shocked silence. Taking advantage of the silence, the soldier went quickly on. "Some of them *will* die tonight, never fear. The Lady and I will plan it, and I myself will see that it is properly done. But forget what has been here proposed, it is simply too chancy!"

The commanding female took over. "Now, brothers and sisters, let us close this meeting with a prayer that Our Lord, the only True God, show us the way to serve Him in the deliverance of our lands from the bloody hands of the godless heathens, and His people and Church from the ancient bondage."

After the round of introductions had been made and all were seated about the table, *Komees* Hari had more wine brought in, along with spiced meats and salty beancakes. Then he and the three newcomers took turns interrogating Bili, sounding out his every feeling, hope, or ambition. They pried into his past, in Harzburk and on campaign, gleaning an encapsulated rendition of ten years of training and warring. That done, *Komees* Djeen put several complicated military problems to him.

For Bili, it was nervewracking to sit there in the hot closeness of the narrow stone chamber, breathing air layered with pipesmoke and lampsmoke, and baring his innermost secrets and desires in response to the probing questions of the four shrewd but increasingly friendly noblemen. Of course, it would have been much quicker and far easier to have conducted the meeting by mindspeak, save for the fact that Lord Drehkos totally lacked that talent.

But Bili consoled himself with the thought that all this was necessary and simply must be borne with as good a face as he could muster. For if these men were to eventually confirm him their Clan Chief and the Thoheeks of Morguhn, they must know him as well as they knew themselves. Only a fool would buy an untested blade, no matter how distinguished its hallmark; and their questions revealed these men to be anything but fools.

It lacked but an hour and a half of midnight when *Komees* Hari arose and stiffly stretched, his joints emitting sharp snaps. "Kindred," he addressed them all, "it is my thought that Bili will be to his clan a chief of famous memory. This night's questioning has proven that he possesses more patience and wisdom than most men of his years. He's a likeable young fellow, even if his manner is a bit stiff and overly formal for this Duchy. But all of us who have soldiered in the Middle Kingdoms can recall the stiff formality of the nobility of those lands, and since Bili was reared and trained there, he is but reflecting his mentors.

"Now, true, he seems a bit bloodthirsty," the *Komees* chuckled, echoed by his brother and *Komees* Djeen, "but it is not mere vicarious pleasure, for he is clearly a proven warrior, and his answers to the problems set to him by Djeen and Ahndros and Vaskos show that he possesses enviable talents as tactician and strategist."

"Plus a thorough understanding of the principles of logistics," put in *Komees* Djeen, holding his specially fashioned winecup with his brass hook, while accenting his words with jabs of the stem of his pipe, "which I wish I'd owned when I was his age. Our Army could use a man like him. And I think he'd enjoy the life of a cavalry officer. Now, if Hwahruhn improves and lives a few years longer . . ."

"Sun and Wind!" Drehkos snorted disgustedly. "For as long as I can remember, Djeen, you've been selling army-life to all and sundry. I vow, in your way you're as bad as

Myros. The moment he claps eyes to a wellformed lad, his mind commences to bed him, while the moment you see one, you're mentally fitting him into a cuirass!"

"Those were most unkind words, Kinsman," came the quiet, gentle, but penetrating voice of the blackclad *Vahrohneeskos* Ahndros. "*Komees* Djeen's Strahteegos Oath binds him for life, and pointing officer-quality men toward our Army is a worthy and laudable act. He it was who persuaded my brothers and me to serve, and I regret none of those years in the Army of the Confederation. Indeed, I would not have returned when I did, had not my inheritance been in jeopardy."

Drehkos made a rude noise. "Strahteegos Oath indeed! Listen you, Ahndros, Djeen's passion to put every man on two legs into armor, and the foxy wiles he uses to achieve that result, far predate his elevation to Strahteegos. Why, thirty-odd years ago he came back here and did his damndest to hornswoggle me and Hari and all the other young Kindred he could catch into that troop of mercenaries he took up to Pitzburk. This, his principal idiosyncrasy, is nothing new or patriotically laudable, young Kinsman!"

His single eye skewering Hari's brother, *Komees* Djeen said slowly and gravely, "And you should have ridden with your brother and me, Drehkos. You'd be a better man for it, today. And you'd have cost your poor, dead father far less expense, heartache, and embarrassment."

Drehkos squirmed and dropped his gaze, his face reddening. "Possibly!" he snapped, shortly. "But we're not gathered here to ruminate on my misspent youth, you know. A chief should have good mindspeak. How is young Bili's? All here know that I possess none myself, so I'll have to take your words for it."

"What say you, Bard Klairuhnz?" inquired Hari. "Your mindspeak seems stronger than average."

Once again, Bili noticed those very odd looks which the Bard and *Vahrohneeskos* Andros—who supposedly had never met prior to this night—were exchanging. He was absolutely certain that the two were mindspeaking, but he could not receive them, try as he might.

"Our young Kinsman is blessed with excellent natural ability," answered Klairuhnz, smiling. "He both transmits and receives well . . . on the basic levels, that is. Of course, with the proper training, he could be even better, stronger."

Stubborn as a dog with a bone in his teeth, *Komees* Djeen immediately snapped, "And he could get that training in our Army, gentlemen, no place is better. Why, there is a special school, in Kehnooryos Atheenahs for the very purpose of developing latent mental abilities. Ask Andros, he attended it."

Komees Hari shook his head. "Desist, Djeen, desist. Considering Hwahruhn's sad state of health and the perils that the Morguhn and Daiviz Kindred presently face, it's out of the question. The place of the Chief's son is here. Until certain matters, which need no repetition, are resolved, *we* will need Bili far more than will the Army . . . and that soon, I fear."

"Vaskos," he turned to his son, "please ask your man to have a servant fetch us a round of brandy, and a draught for himself as well. He's been a good watchdog for our door, this night. When we've had our tipple, Kinsmen, I think we should to bed. Tomorrow will commence a very busy week for most of us."

Rising to his feet, Bili chose his words cautiously. "Kinsman Hari, please do not misunderstand me and do not read into what I am about to say meanings which are certainly not intended. It is not that I scorn the gracious hospitality of your fine hall, nor that I fear to sleep under your protection. On the contrary . . ."

But the laughter of old *Komees* Djeen brought him up short. The retired officer wiped at his eye, admonishing, "Oh, Bili, Bili, lad, we must, I fear, reeducate you. Your Kinsman Hari is no thin-skinned northern princeling, ready to shed blood or make war over some fancied slight or imagined insult.

"He—all of us—are your Kindred, son, and we're a blunt, outspoken people. If you really want to ride home at this hagridden hour, by Sun and Wind, come right out and say so! Not that I think it's basically a good idea for you, the hope of us all, to ride all those miles alone, on a dark night, as unsafe as our roads have been of late . . . nor with all that seems afoot in this Duchy.

"I want no harm to come to you, boy. Much as I love your father, I will say that he's been a poor chief in many ways, too lax and soft on men who deserve, have long deserved, a strong and pitiless hand. From what I know of you, what more I've learned of you tonight, you'll be the kind of chief your father should have been, the kind of chief your grandfather—Sacred Sun shine always on his memory—was.

"Your dear mothers should have sent a few of their Freefighters with you today. They know, even if you are too lately come to know, that the night roads are no longer safe for Kindred, in either our duchy or in that of our western neighbor, Chief Sidnee of Vawn. Now, if Hari had taken my advice and hired a few Freefighters himself, he could loan you a proper escort, but . . ."

Djeen's quoted advice was obviously a sore point with his host, for the short, stocky *Komees* immediately lashed back angrily, "Fah! Just because you've made of your hall a small fortress does not signify that the rest of us must hire on a host of useless mouths, men whose only accomplishments are their expertise at eating and drinking and gambling and wenching . . ."

"*And* fighting!" snapped *Komees* Djeen, unfazed by the other's anger.

His face beetred and his big fists clenched, Hari opened his mouth to say more, but Ahndros quietly said, "Kinsman Bili will not be alone, Kindred; for I too am of a mind to ride to Morguhn Hall tonight."

The *Komeesee* burst into laughter, their shouting match forgotten. Vaskos showed every tooth and Drehkos chuckled. "Soooo, Ahndros, *that* is why you wear that new velvet suit and those new boots! By Wind, Kinsman, you shine like a new moon. Take warning, if *Vahrohnos* Myros sees you looking so handsome, he'll have you bedded and buggered before you can blink!"

Komees Djeen's laughter ceased abruptly and he spoke in a voice edged with steel. "Sun and Wind grant that I live to see the day that Myros makes advances toward Ahndros. Oh-ho, that will be a sight to see! For years that degenerate boarhog has been in sore need of gelding!"

Vahrohneeskos Ahndros said nothing in response to the jesting. He but sat, sipping at his wine and smiling now and again. All that Bili had learned of the modest man's military exploits this night had come from others, mostly from *Komees* Djeen and Vaskos Daiviz. But before any word had been spoken, from their first handclasp and mindspeak, Bili had known Ahndros for what he was: a quiet, unassuming and basically gentle man; but, withal, a born warrior and warleader, who would be the best of allies or the most dangerous of foemen when swords were out. And women had told him that these bravest of men were right oft the tenderest of lovers. Bili thought that Mother Mahrnee had chosen well.

Bard Klairuhnz interrupted the rough banter. "Kinsmen, did I hear someone say that Hail Morguhn, your Clanbard, would be quartering the next week at Morguhn Hall? If so, I'd like the hospitality of Kinsman Bili, for I try to meet every bard I may."

Bili smiled, even while wondering what might be the mysterious "bard's" real purpose for riding with him this night. "Of course, Kinsman Klairuhnz, you are more than welcome at my father's hall."

"Well," grumbled *Komees* Djeen finally. "I still don't like it, but three armed men—no, four, I'd forgot your retainer Ahndros; he doesn't look like much of a fighter, but we'll at least give him the appearance with a helmet and a spear—you should scare off any skulkers. And I'll have a couple of my troopers ride along with you, 'til you're over the bridge and beyond the woods, anyhow."

Turning to their host, he said, "Hari, unlock your cabinets and let's get these lads and Kinsman Klairuhnz fitted with armor. If the party looks strong and sufficiently well-armed, chances are there'll be no attack on them. As the adage of our ancestors had it: It takes the courage of a wolf to attack a guarded herd. And we're dealing with only jackals here.

"Kinsman Vaskos, please ask your father's servants to saddle our Kinsmen's horses and that big mule Ahndros's man rides. Don't fret about my troopers, mind you, they'll saddle their own."

The troopers finished saddling all of the horses. Alternately, *Komees* Hari bawled the names of the missing servants and looked fit to die of embarrassment. *Komees* Djeen did not miss the opportunity to make the point that if Hari had had a few Freefighters of his own guarding the hall exits, the servants should have played merry hell getting out of the compound this late. At that, anger replaced all other emotions in Hari.

"Damn you, Djeen! *My* hall is not an armed camp! *My* people and servants love me and mine, and I need no barbarian jailers to lock them up of a night, nor to oversee them in the day!"

Geros, Ahndros's retainer, led out his master's horse and the Vahrohneeskos swung into the saddle, settling weightlessly, despite the added encumbrance of the three-quarter armor and thick, leathern gambeson into which *Komees* Djeen had chivvied the three of them, ere he'd allow them out of the hall. The rest of the party were already mounted and quaffing stirrupcups of cool wine laced with brandy, prepared by Vaskos and served by him and his orderly, Frahnkos.

At the open gate, Bili reined about and leaned from his kak to exchange final handclasps with Hari, Drehkos, Vaskos, and, lastly, *Komees* Djeen.

Speaking rapidly and in a low-voice, the old Strahteegos told him, "I want to see you again, alive, Bili, so do you what I say. I think we're all in far more danger than we now know. I'll keep all here awake and armed until Dzhool and Shahrl get back. In those damned woods, form you a tight column and take the track at a brisk trot. If you let them string out, it could be the death of you or Ahndee or both, and . . ." Drehkos strode over, laughing. "Let be, Djeen, let be. They've a long ride before them. Surely you can find a better time to lecture on cavalry tactics?"

CHAPTER V

Once they were clear of the gate, Ahndros trotted his silvergrey gelding up abreast of Bili and mindspoke. "*Komees* Djeen is a fine old man, Bili. I love and respect him more than any living man."

"It is clear that he returns your love tenfold," replied Bili.

Ahndros continued, "That's why it pains me to say what I now must. Uncle Djeen dearly loves all aspects of soldiering, especially the fighting. He is constantly expecting—eagerly looking for, really—brigands or wouldbe assassins around every turn and behind every tree.

"Now true, things are not all sweetness and light in our lands. But it is my opinion that we let them strap us into these 'Pitzburk steamers' and are a party to robbing the sleep from those Freefighters back there, to no just purpose."

"You expect no attack tonight, then?" Bili inquired.

Ahndros sighed aloud, though still mindspeaking. "Oh, anything is possible, I suppose. Sure it is that the roads aren't so safe as once they were . . . not for Kindred, at least. Perhaps Uncle Djeen is right. After all, his intuition won many a battle for the Confederation."

The little party rode on, between the mile or more of roadside fences, intended to keep deer and wandering livestock out of the choice pasturage reserved for *Komees* Hari's herds. The black-on-black outlines of the rails made it easier to stay on the road, for only rarely did a winking star or a slice of moon manage to find a way through the squadrons of scudding clouds.

At a horsesaving walk, the double column followed the wellkept road up and down the gentle, rolling hills it traversed. Bili found the fresh night air a pleasant contrast to the thick smokiness of *Komees* Hari's study. The cooling breeze which blew across their path bore away most of the dust the hooves raised from the roadway.

Bili sent his reception ranging ahead and to the flanks, striving to pick up any trace of hostile mindpatterns, but the conversations of the four men riding behind him proved too distracting. Geros and Klairuhnz were swapping anecdotes and bawdy tales, while the two big, rawboned troopers chattered continually in some alien tongue. It sounded, to Bili, a bit like the nasal language called *Kweebehkyuhn,* spoken by some tribes of those odd folk who dwelt north and west of the Sea of Eeree . . . but perhaps it was really *Nyahgraheekos,* which sounded similar.

Other than the conversations, the creak of the saddles, and jingling of spurs and bridlechains, the rattling of armor and the thudding of the hooves were all the sounds which disturbed the nightshrouded land. Far away, across the lea, a dogfox barked, and closer at hand came the cry of a hunting owl. But Bili could range no nearby danger, so he relaxed and mindspoke Ahndros.

"Komees Djeen sometimes calls you 'Ahndee.' May I do so?"

"Why, of course, Bili, I much prefer the Kindred form to the Ehleen."

"Thank you then, Ahndee," said Bili silently. "Let me ask you, when you have your city and lands in order, do you intend to return to the Army? You could have a splendid career, you know; a Subkeeleeohstos of your age could reasonably expect to be strahteegos by his fortieth year, if not before, and even I know that's a damned rare accomplishment."

But Ahndee shook his head. "No, Bili, that phase of my life is done forever. I may journey to the capital occasionally, for I've many friends there; but mostly I want to attend to my lands and people and lead as quiet and nonviolent a life as circumstances will allow. I don't enjoy soldiering, Bili."

"Then why did you join the Army at all?" queried Bili.

Ahndee breathed another sigh. "I'll try to explain.

"Bili, my Uncle Djeen was worshiped by me and my two brothers for the most of our lives. He was our ideal as we were growing up, the very epitome of stalwart manhood. For some reason, none of his wives or women could ever give him children—his present daughter is adopted, his new wife's by her first husband—and he undertook the virtual rearing of Oomros and Gaibrios and me, when he was home between campaigns or to recover from wounds. He was patient and gentle and loving, honorable and honest, cleanly in his habits, temperate in his few vices, and capable of astounding feats of self-discipline.

"Bili, what know you of my late father?"

Bili squirmed uncomfortably in his saddle. In the eight years before he had left for the north, he had heard more than he now wished to remember of *Vahrohneeskos* Ehlmos. "Well, uh . . . Ahndee, I, uh . . . Let's see . . . your House follows the Old Ehleen ways, but, ahhh . . . as your grandfather had no sons . . ."

"Oh, Bili," Ahndee expostulated impatiently. "Spit it out! You're not going to offend *me* by repeating truths known to all the Duchy. Yes, my House followed the Old Ehleen practices—both the good and the bad, the tasteful and the distasteful, the honorable and the dishonorable. My grandfather wed very late, and then only because the Council and your grandfather forced him to it. It is far from certain that he actually sired my mother. And I rejoice in that uncertainty, Bili, for I'd hate to be sure that the old degenerate's tainted blood runs in my veins. Sun and Wind know the mere suspicion that I am my *father's* son is hard enough to live with.

"As for the thing who called himself my father, Bili, what know you of him?"

"Right little, Ahndee," Bili answered, and could not help adding, "And none of that little good, I'm afraid."

Ahndee immediately reassured him, saying, "I meant what I said before, Bili. Unpleasant as it is, the truth does not offend me. Now, what do you know of the late *Vahrohneeskos* Ehlmos?"

"If you insist, Kinsman." Bili set his jaw. "It is said that right often he appeared in public garbed in your mother's clothing and jewels, with his lips and eyes and cheeks painted. It is also said that, after your mother's death, he coerced an Ehleen priest into reciting marriage rites over him and . . . and a blacksmith's apprentice, that the *Vahrohneeskos*'s bridal costume cost near five hundred thrahkmehs. It is said that all his court were compelled to witness the events of his bridal night and . . . and that . . . that your father wept and wailed and . . . and whimpered like a maiden, when first the apprentice took him.

"But, Ahndee," he hurriedly added, "these are but things I have heard said over the years, mostly servants' gossip, probably."

"No, Bili, truth, all of it excepting the first part. My mother was a tiny woman, her clothing would never have fitted the *Vahrohneeskos*. No, his female clothing was all made expressly for him, tailored to his measure. You see, he . . ." Ahndee broke off as Bili suddenly halted Mahvros.

They were at the crest of a low hillock, beyond which the road ran arrowstraight to the wagonwide, wooden bridge. Beyond the bridge, crouching like some monstrous beast of nightmare, loomed the black forest.

And danger lurked within that forest, this Bili knew! Although that danger's emanations lay just beyond the range of his perceptions, still could he sense its presence. But his far-range perceptivity was very tricky; Bili would have been the first to admit to that fact. The hostile impressions given him by some something lodged amongst that gloomy host of thickholed trees could easily be a short-tempered boar or a hungry bear or both together.

Bard Klairuhnz walked his highspirited mount up to the slope, reining in beside Bili, and the three battlewise veterans briefly studied the bridge, its approaches, and the deep, swiftflowing stream whose high banks it joined. The moon had once more freed herself of the shrouding clouds and her pale radiance allowed Bili his first glimpse of the Bard since they had quit the torchlit courtyard of Horse Hall. Though Klairuhnz smiled warmly—supposedly at Bili—his black eyes were on Ahndee, and Bili once more had that weird feeling that the two were somehow communicating . . . and that feeling did nothing to detract from his general uneasiness.

Partially to soothe himself, he uncased his axe, for he always felt secure and happy with the hidewound haft in his hand. That done, he hung the bared weapon from a heavy hook let into the flaring pommel of his kak, dismounted, and loosened, then lengthened, his stirrup leathers. When he remounted, he was no longer sitting Mahvros—the great beast, recognizing the familiar preparations for imminent combat, stamping and snorting his joyful anticipation. Most of his weight was now on his booted feet.

Ahndee's handsome face mirrored his incredulity. "Why in the world did you do that, Bili? It looks to be damned unsteady and uncomfortable."

Bili laughed merrily. "You're a swordsman, Kinsman. Were you an axeman now—and with your build, you'd be a natural axewielder, you know!—you'd not need to ask." Seeing that his companion still did not understand, Bili went on patiently, "What's the weight of your sword, Ahndee? Three pounds? Five? My good axe weighs thirteen Harzburk pounds, the equal of more than a dozen of your Ehleen keelohs, so the arms and shoulders are not enough. To use it properly, to get a swing powerful enough to stave in armor, requires the muscles of the lower back and the legs as well."

Ahndee still looked a bit dubiously at Bili's "seat." "If you say so, Bili. But how do you manage to stay astride, if you have to move faster than a slow trot?"

Bili's white teeth flashed in the moonlight. "That, Kinsman, takes practice!"

The young axeman would have taken the lead into the place of danger, had not Ahndee, Klairuhnz, and the two Freefighters argued him down. So when the column trotted toward the bridge, Bili was third in line, with Klairuhnz ahead and Dzhool, the younger of *Komees* Djeen's troopers, at point; behind rode Ahndee, then Geros, then the trooper Shahrl.

The more closely they approached the forest, the stronger grew Bili's dreadful apprehension. Now he knew that they were certainly riding into a battle, and he so mindspoke both Ahndee and Klairuhnz.

Awe in his voice, Ahndee silently asked, "You can *far-gather*, then, Bili? That's a rare and precious ability. We were told of it at the Confederation Mindspeak Academy, of course; but not even the instructors had ever met a man or woman who actually possessed it! Can you tell how many foemen, and how far ahead they be?"

"No," Bili admitted. "Never have I been able to judge numbers, but we are near and drawing nearer."

The thick old planks of the bridge boomed hollowly under ironshod hooves; then they were into the forest. Bili found it far less dark within than it had appeared from without. Except for the oakgrown fringes, the growth was principally tall, old pines, unbranching for many feet above roadlevel. The wan moonlight filtered through the needles, making for a dim visibility.

The road ran straight for a few dozen yards, then began a gradual ascent and slight curvature to the right, following the lower reaches of a brushgrown hillock. They splashed through a tiny rill, which fed down into a small swamp before it joined the larger stream. Beyond the rill, the road commenced another slow curve, this one to the left. As they descended the reverse slope, the moon dove for cover, and Bili's hackles rose. The unseen danger was near, terribly near!

"SOON!" he urgently mindspoke Ahndee and Klairuhnz, while bringing his axe up, so that its fearsome, doublebitted head rested against his armored right shoulder. Dropping his reins over the pommelknob—in battle, he guided Mahvros solely by mindspeak and kneepressure, not that the battlewise stallion required a great deal of guidance—he lowered and securely locked into place the slitted halfvisor which protected the eyes and nose. By that time, the peril lay so very near, pressed so heavily, that he could hardly bear it.

"NOW!" He beamed with mindblasting intensity. *"IT IS ALL AROUND US!"*

Ahndee and Klairuhnz drew their blades, and the *zweep* of steel leaving scabbard alerted the troopers, who bared their own weapons. Geros awkwardly gripped and regripped the shaft of the widebladed boarspear in his sweaty hand. He knew next to nothing of arms and their use, and showed it.

Up the slope to their left, the trees abruptly began to thin . . . and the fickle moon chose that moment to commence a slow emergence.

There was a scuffling noise at the head of the column, a strangled grunt, followed almost immediately by a horse's shrill scream of pain and terror, then the unmistakable clash-clanking of an armored body falling to the ground. And the moon came fully out.

Bili could see the trooper, Dzhool, twitching on the roadway. A stocky, blackbearded man had a foot on the dying Freefighter's chest, frantically striving to jerk his spearpoint from the body. He never got the weapon free, for Bard Klairuhnz kneed his chestnut forward; his long saber swept up, then blurred down. The bearded head, still wearing its oldfashioned helmet, clattered across the road and into the weeds. The trunk stood a brief moment, then pitched forward over its victim's body, shortened neck spouting ropy streams of blood.

From around the far side of the screaming, hamstrung lead horse rushed another of the attackers, lacking either helm or armor, but swinging up a short, widebladed infantry sword. This man was as stocky as the first, but beardless and greyhaired, his thin lips peeled back in a grimace which revealed his rotten teeth. There was fresh blood on his swordblade and he ran directly at Bili, shouting something in Old Ehleeneekos.

Ahndee watched Bili—with seeming effortlessness handling his long, massive weapon with one hand—catch the slash on the steel shaft of his axe and allow the blade's own momentum to propel it into the deep notch between head and haft. A single twist of Bili's thick wrist tore the hilt from the old man's grip and sent it spinning. The spike above the two axebits was jammed deep into the ancient's chest, ere that sword had come to ground.

Dead Dzhool's crippled mount was still screaming. Geros, too, began to scream, so terrified that he could form no words, but wail and point the boarspear up at the brushy slope. There a rank of riders, at least a dozen of them, armed and armored, was coming from the trees which had concealed them.

"BACK!" roared Klairunhz. "There's too many to fight here! Back to the bridge!" Setting words to actions, he reined his mount about and set off in the wake of Shahrl, Geros, and Ahndee.

Bili stayed only long enough to split the skull of the suffering horse. Then he set off toward the bridge, just as the line of mounted ambushers came tilting down the rise. This granted Bili a closer look; his experienced eyes informed him that though numerous—nearer a score than a dozen—the charging horsemen were not nearly so well armed as they had at first seemed.

All had swords of one kind or another, and a few even bore them as if they understood them, but the uniformity ended there. A big man in the lead had a full panoply of threequarter armor and it looked to be decent-quality plate. The remainder might have been outfitted from a hundred years of battlefield pickings. Their helms were of every description. One man wore nought save a dented breastplate, another had squeezed into a shirt of rusty scalemail. Two or three went in loricated jerkins, one in a cuirass of boiled leather, another in an old, threadbare brigandine. Bili thought that the ruffianly crew looked the part of the brigands they probably were.

Mahvros's powerful body responded to Bili's urgings and big steelshod hooves struck sparks from the pebbly roadbed. The black stallion splashed through the little rill, and then they were descending the road's first curve. Suddenly, twenty yards ahead, riders emerged from among the treetrunks to block the way. A shaft of moonlight silvered their bared blades.

At a walk or a trot, Geros Lahvoheetos's big mule was a good mount, but the animal's ragged gallop was a jarring, toothloosening ordeal. Despite this, Geros was spurraking the roan barrel and screaming for greater speed.

The bridge now lay behind them and the road traversed was the wellkept one, flanked by *Komees* Hari's fences. From back there, came the sudden commencement of a blacksmith symphony of steel on steel, the metallic clangs punctuated by the shouts and shrieks of man and horse. Geros's own screams then froze in his throat and he could only sob out his terror, while great tears furrowed his dusty cheeks.

His employer had bidden him ride hard for Horse Hall. He was to inform *Komees* Djeen that the party was under attack from at least half a score of armored and mounted bravos, and they were withdrawing to make their stand at the bridge. He was to add that one mercenary was slain; and that *Thoheek*'s son Bili had lingered at the original ambush site to dispatch a wounded horse and was now missing.

Had his overwhelming fear not occupied every nook and cranny of his mind, Geros would have been thanking every god he had never heard of that he had been chosen messenger and sent away from the scene of battle. For though he had quickly come to love his gentle, patient, softspoken young employer, he knew himself sufficiently to realize that in an actual fight, he would probably have deserted him.

He would have consoled himself, of course, by rationalizing that he had not been retained on account of his weapons skill, of which he had none, but simply as a bodyservant and occasional musician, at both of which trades he excelled. But he could have continued neither with an arm lopped off or a foot of sharp steel rammed into his body. And this last thought would have brought up his gorge and he would have silently damned himself for a despicable craven. He had always secretly feared that he was a coward, never having been in a position to prove himself one way or another.

He heard approaching hoofbeats ahead, and as he crested the second hillock from the hall, he saw the source—a galloping horse and three armed men, one astride and the other two grasping the stirrup leathers and running alongside. Before he could think of what to say or do, even rein his mule, the mounted man shouted.

"It's the renegade *Vahrohneeskos*'s lackey. Kill him!"

Geros still bore the spear, despite his terror and flight, principally because he knew it to be the property of a nobleman and was afraid of the consequences of losing it. But he was completely ignorant of how such a weapon was employed. So, gripping the thick ash shaft near the ferrule, he let go his reins and aimed a twohanded swing at the oncoming horseman, seeking but to knock the man out of his saddle, that he might have a clear road to the safety of Horse Hall.

The mule careered downslope, at a flatout run. And the other rider spurred forward, leaving the two footmen behind. This man had been clandestinely drilling for over a year and had absorbed enough to extend his ancient saber at arm's length, seeking to spit Geros on the point. But the spear was more than twice as long as his curved saber and, thanks to the moonlight and the flitting shadows and swirling dust, he never saw that spear until it was far too late.

Poor, frightened Geros had completely forgotten that his long cudgel mounted a wide, leafshaped steel head. His wild swing missed his adversary—he had swung too soon—but that deadly point chanced to be in just the proper place at just the proper time for the swordsman to spit himself upon it. It would be fair to say that neither was the more surprised!

The combined impetus of mule and horse lifted the pierced man shrieking from his saddle, and his horse ran from under him, dropping him to the roadway. The shock of the unexpected impalement almost drove Geros over his own cantle; only his fear-locked thighs retained him his seat. Unable to release his grip on the spearshaft, he thought his shoulder must be disjointed, in the splitsecond before the bloodslimed blade came free of its lodging with a sucking sound.

The two footmen just stood in the road, their weapons dangling beside them, shocked beyond words at what they had witnessed. Secret drills in benighted meadows and brave words spoken in the dark were one thing, but coughing up your lifeblood on a moonlit roadway was something entirely different! They still had not ordered their benumbed brains sufficiently to run, when Geros was on them.

The big mule's shoulder struck the foremost, sprawling him backward, directly in the animal's path. The last thing he ever saw was the immense, looming hoof that shattered his face and crushed his skull.

The second man stood on Geros's right. Clumsily, he brought up his old sword, wishing less to fight than simply to fend off that horrible spear, already wetly gleaming with his friend's blood. Again swinging twohanded, Geros's spearshaft again missed its target . . . but the tip of the knife-edged blade connected. The footman dropped his sword and clutched at his slashed throat, his last screams bubbling out his severed windpipe.

Reins flying free, its rider in a state of shock, the mule pounded into the brightlit courtyard and would probably have kept going until it struck a wall, had not one of *Komees* Djeen's troopers run and leaped to grasp the curbchain and halt the beast. Geros let go the spear and slid from the mule's back, but had to clutch tightly at the saddle when his legs refused to support him.

Komees Djeen crossed from the hall at a limping run. He was encased in a suit of plate, a golden cat crouched atop his helm and another enameled on the wide baldric supporting his heavy broadsword. His gauntleted hand crushingly gripped Geros's trembling shoulder.

"What is it, man? What has happened? Dammit, speak!"

But the trooper who had stopped the mule spoke first. "He's been fighting, My Lord Count. Look at this spear, there's fresh blood half down the shaft."

"Brandy!" The old man snapped over his shoulder, to no one in particular. Then turning back to Geros, his tone became solicitous. "Had to fight your way through them, did you, comrade? I must confess I misjudged you earlier, thought you a man of no mettle. Glad to see I was wrong.

"It requires a high degree of courage to do what you did, lad—ride off alone, though hostile forces, to fetch succor for your comrades. I always feel privileged to meet men of your rare kind. The Confederation never has enough of you."

Had Geros been able to let go his hold on the saddle, he would have pinched himself. He was certain that he must be dreaming. Such accolade for Geros-the-coward, from so great and famous a noble warrior, must surely be a dream. He opened his mouth, tried hard to speak, but his still-constricted and brickdry throat emitted only a croak.

"No, no, comrade," *Komees* Djeen gently patted his shoulder. "Don't try to talk 'til you've had of your tipple."

As soon as he had recovered from the coughing fit engendered by the strong, hastily gulped brandy, Geros gasped out his message, and the courtyard began to buzz like an overturned beehive. Already saddled horses were led out and the girths tightened, bows strung, weapons hefted, and last-minute adjustments made to belts, stirrups, and armor.

Shortly, *Komees* Djeen's small command galloped out of the gate. Intensive search had failed to find any of *Komees* Hari's servants, so there were but nineteen riders in the column—the four noblemen, the orderlies of Djeen and Vaskos, Drehkos's bodyservant, and his big, mountain-barbarian bodyguard, ten scaleshirted Freefighters . . . and Geros.

"We'll surely need every fighter, comrade," *Komees* Djeen had declared, while two troopers buckled Geros's cuirass, draped a baldric over his shoulder, and handed him a fresh spear. "Especially a gutsy man like you. Were you a soldier, I'd see you wear a Cat for this night's work!"

CHAPTER VI

Bili mindspoke Mahvros, "Faster, brother! Be ready to fight."

The huge, black horse quickened his gait and beamed his approval, one of his principal joys being the stamping of the life from anything that got in his way. Raising his head, he voiced a shrill, equine challenge, then bore down on his promised victims.

One man and horse went down in a squealing, screaming, hoof-flailing tangle, while Bili took a ringing swordcut on the side of his helm in passing. Still shrilling his challenge, Mahvros came to a rearing halt, pivoted, and returned to savage the downed horse and rider, while Bili axed the other man out of the saddle with a single, businesslike stroke. The stallion was able to experience the brief elation of feeling manribs splinter under his hooves, before Bili urged him back toward the bridge.

Scores of hooves were pounding close behind him, when he cleared the last of the trees to see Ahndee and Klairuhnz, their blades gleaming, sitting their mounts knee-to-knee, a few paces onto the span. Three yards behind them, the trooper had uncased and strung his short bow, nocked an arrow, and calmly awaited the appearance of a target.

"Bili!" shouted Ahndee exuberantly. "Sun and Wind be thanked! We'd thought you slain." He started to back his gelding, that Bili might have his place.

But Bili signed him to stay, positioning Mahvros a little

ahead of the others. "This will be better," he stated shortly, not seeing the smile they exchanged at his automatic assumption of command.

The trooper proved himself an expert archer, putting his shaft cleanly into the eye of the first pursuer to gallop out of the forest. His second arrow pinned an unarmored thigh to a saddletree. He nocked a third, drew . . . and his bowstring snapped! Cursing sulfurously in several languages, he cast away the now useless hornbow, drew his saber, and ranged up close behind Ahndee.

The next four attackers took a brief moment to form up, then launched a charge, apparently expecting their prey to remain in place and wait their pleasure. They did not live long enough to recover from the countercharge!

The leading attacker held up his shield to fend off Bili's axe, while he aimed a hacking cut at Mahvros's thick neck. The stout target crumpled like wet paper and the axeblade bit completely through, deep into the arm beneath, the force of the buffet hurling the man down to a singularly messy death, amid the stamping hooves.

Mahvros roughly shouldered the riderless horse aside, while Bili glanced around, seeking another opponent. At that very moment Ahndee was thrusting the watered-steel blade of his broadsword deep into the vitals of his adversary and Klairuhnz was obviously more than a match for his shaggy opponent. But the Freefighter had troubles aplenty. First his bowstring, and now his saber had broken, leaving him but a bare foot of pointless blade. With this stub, he was fighting a desperate defensive action.

In one mighty leap, Mahvros was alongside the ruffian's mount. Shortening his grip on his axe, Bili jammed the spike into a side made vulnerable by a wide gap between the breast and back plates of an ill-fitting cuirass. Shrieking a curse, the mortally wounded man turned in his saddle to rain a swift succession of swordcuts on Bili's helm and shoulders. While the Pitzburk turned every blow, Bili was unable to retaliate, his axe being almost useless at such breast-to-breast encounters.

Unexpectedly, the man hunched and began to gag and retch, spewing up quantities of frothy-pink blood. At this, the Freefighter reined closer, used his piece of saber to slash the dying man's swordknot, then neatly decapitated the brigand with his own antique blade.

They had almost regained the bridge when the van of the main force caught up to them. First to fall was the rearmed Freefighter, his scaleshirt unable to protect his back from a nailstudded club.

Bili's better armor turned a determined spearthurst, before he axed an arm from his spearman. Then he turned Mahvros and, straightening his arms, swung his bloody axe in several wide arcs before him. He struck nothing, but did achieve the desired effect of momentarily halting most of the oncoming force and granting Ahndee and Klairuhnz a few precious moments to regain the bridge.

Bili failed to see the man who galloped in from his left, but Mahvros did not.

With the speed of a striking serpent, he swung about and sank his big teeth into the flesh of the smaller horse. The little mare was not a warhorse, and she had no slightest intention of remaining in proximity to a huge, maddened stallion. Taking the bit firmly in her teeth, she raced back into the forest, bearing her shouting, cursing, reinsawing rider only as far as the low-hanging branch, which swept him from her back and stretched him senseless on the sward.

Mahvros's forehooves were already booming on the bridgetimbers when a hardflung throwingaxe caromed off Bili's helm, nearly deafening him and filling his head with a tight red-blackness shot with dazzling-white stars. Only instinct kept him in the saddle; Mahvros, well-trained and intelligent animal that he was, continued on to the proper place, then wheeled about just ahead of Ahndee and Klairuhnz.

Reaching forward, Ahndee grabbed Bili's limp arm and shook him. "Are you all right, Bili? Are you hurt?" he shouted anxiously.

Then he turned to Klairuhnz. "Your help, My Lord, he's all but unconscious. Let's get him behind us, ere those bastards cut him down."

Bili could hear all and could feel movements on either side of him, but neither his lips nor his limbs would obey him. Fuzzily, he pondered on why *Vahrohneeskos* Ahndee would have addressed a mere roving bard as his lord.

Holding at the bridge where a flank attack was impossible had been a good idea. The blades of Ahndee and Klairuhnz wove a deadly pattern, effectively barring their foemen access to the dazed and helpless Bili, now drooping in his saddle. Thanks to the narrowness of the span, only two men at a time could attack the defenders, thus nullifying their numerical superiority. On a man-to-man basis, the ill-armed crew were no match for experienced warriors. The length of the bridge, from the forest side to the center, was soon goreslimed and littered with dropped weapons and hacked, hoofmarked corpses.

But the repeated assaults had taken other toll. Ahndee sat in agony, his left arm uselessly dangling at his side. He had used its armored surface to ward off a direct blow from a huge and weighty club, while he slashed the clubman's unprotected throat. He was certain that the concussion of that blow had broken the arm. Klairuhnz's horse now lay dead and the Bard stood astride the body. He had hopefully mindspoken Mahvros, but the stallion's refusal had been final. He had been promised dire consequences should he attempt to either unseat Mahvros's hurt brother or take his place on the big black.

Bili regained his senses just in time to see Klairuhnz sustain a vicious cut on the side of his neck and fall, blood spurting over his shoulderplates. Roaring *"UP HARZBURK!"* through force of habit, Bili kneed Mahvros forward and plugged the gap, admonishing the horse not to step on the fallen man. A swing of his axe crushed both the helmet and the skull of Klairuhnz's killer. As the man pitched from his saddle, Bili belatedly recognized the face. It was that of Hofos, *Komees* Hari's majordomo!

Then there were two more enemy horsemen on the bridge before him. But this time it was Ahndee who was reeling on his kak, unable to do more than offer a rapidly weakening defense. Bili disliked attacking a horse, but the circumstances left him no option. He rammed his axe spike into the rolling eye of his opponent's mount, and in the brief respite afforded him while the death-agonized beast proceeded to buck its rider over the low railing and into the cold creek, he swung his axe into the unarmored chest of Ahndee's adversary. Deep went that fearsome blade, biting through hide jerkin and shirt and skin and flesh and bone and into the quivering heart itself!

Someone in the decreasing group between the bridge and the forest cast a javelin and Mahvros took it in the thick muscles of his off shoulder. He screamed his pain and shock and would have reared, had Bili's mindspeak not restrained him. Grimly, the young man dismounted and gently withdrew the blessedly unbarbed head. Backing the big horse, he turned him, beaming, "Go back to the hall, Mahvros."

"Mahvros still can fight, Brother!" the black balked stubbornly.

"I know that my brother can still fight." Bili mindspoke with as much patience as he could show. "But that wound is deep. If I stayed on your back, you might be permanently crippled." Thinking quickly, he added, "Besides, the other man can fight no longer and must be returned to the hall. A horse of your intelligence is needed to keep this stupid gelding moving, yet see that it does not move too fast so that the man falls off."

Bili was not exaggerating. Ahndee had dropped both sword and reins, and nothing save the high cantle and pommel of his war kak were keeping his limp, unconscious body on his horse. Bili grasped the grey's bridle, faced him about, slapped his rump, and shouted. Even so, the grey made to stop at the end of the bridge, but a sharp nip of Mahvros's yellow teeth changed his mind.

Laying down both axe and javelin, Bili grasped Klairuhnz under the arms and dragged him back from the windrow of the dead men and horses, propping him against the rail. Odd, he thought vaguely, I think he's still alive. He should be well dead, by now, considering where the sword caught him. . . .

Striding back, he picked up the short, heavy dart, drew back his brawny arm, then chose a target and made a running cast. One of the men with only a breastplate was adjusting his stirrup when the missile took him in the small of the back, tearing through his guts and far enough out from his belly to prick his horse when he stumbled against its flank. Scream of horse almost drowned out scream of man. The riderless mount galloped for the forest and most of the remaining ruffians made move to follow.

But a big, spikebearded man headed them off and, beating at them with the flat of a broadsword, drove them back and commenced to harangue them. Bili, leaning on his gory axe amid the dead men whom he expected to soon join, could pick out words or detached phrases of the angrily shouted monologue, despite the fact that he had not heard Old Ehleeneekos spoken in ten years.

". . . cowards . . . to fear only one, dismounted man . . . creatures of filth . . . gotten on filtheating sows by spineless cur dogs . . . gain your freedom? . . . lead all men to the True Faith? . . . treasure and women? . . . Salvation . . . killing heathens . . ."

Bili shook his head, hoping to clear it of the remaining dizziness. A true product of his race and upbringing, he had no fear of death. He was a bit sorry that it was to come so early in his life, but then every warrior faced his last battle sooner or later. He would have liked to have seen his father and his sweet mothers just once more, but it would rejoice them when they learned that he had fallen in honor, his foemen's blood clotting his axe from spikepoint to butt. And his brother Djehf, six months his junior, would certainly make a good Chief and *Thoheeks* of Morguhn, maybe even a better one than he would have made.

"DIRTMEN!" He shouted derisively at the band of ruffians. "Rapists of ewes and she-goats! Your fellow bastards here are lonely. Are you going to come join them, or are you going home to bugger your own infant sons? That's an old Ehleen custom, isn't it? Along with eating dung?"

He carried on in the same vein, each succeeding insult more repugnant and offensive than its predecessor. Their leader wisely held his tongue, hoping that Bili's sneering contumely would arouse an aggressive spark in his battered band where his own oration had failed.

At length, one of the tatterdemalions was stung to the quick. Shouting maniacally, waving his aged saber, he spurred his horse at the lone figure on the bridge. Bili stood his ground; to the watching men it appeared that he was certain to be ridden down. But Bili had positioned himself cunningly, and he judged the oncoming rider to be something less than an accomplished horseman.

The horse had to jump in order to clear the two dead horses blocking the direct route to the axeman. Before the rider could recover enough of his balance to use his sword, Bili had let his axe go to swing by its wrist thong, grabbed a sandaled foot and a thick, hairy leg, and heaved him over the other side of his mount!

Dropping his sword and squalling in terror, the Ehleen clawed frantically for a grip on the bridgerail. He missed and commenced a despairing howl which was abruptly terminated when his hurtling body struck the swiftflowing water. He had been one of the "lucky ones," arrayed in an almost complete set of threequarter plate. Since he could not swim anyway, he sank like a stone.

But Bili had not watched. No sooner was the man out of the saddle, than he who had unseated him was in it, trying to turn the unsettled and unfamiliar animal in time to meet the fresh attackers he could hear pounding up. Hear . . . but not see, for once more the sick, tight dizziness was attempting to claim his senses. When at last he got the skittish horse facing the forest, it was to dimly perceive the backs of the motley pack of skulkers pounding toward the forest, a small shower of arrows falling amongst them, the shafts glinting as they crossed a vagrant beam of moonlight.

Bili's brain told his arm to lift the axe, his legs to urge the new horse on in pursuit of the fleeing ruffians . . . vainly. His legs might have ceased to exist, while his axe now seemed to weigh tons. The weight was just too much and he let it go, then pitched out of the lowcut saddle to land on the narrow railing above the deep, icy water.

Hari and Drehkos caught the senseless body just in time to prevent Bili from joining his latest victim on the bed of the stream. While *Komees* Djeen led his men on the trail of the fleeing force, the brothers bore the *Thoheek*'s son to where Vaskos and his orderly, Frahnkos, were tending Ahndee. When Bili's battered helmet was removed, it was found to be filled with both old and fresh blood from a nasty scalp wound. Nor was that the extent of his hurts. Once his body lay prone, a stream of blood crept from the top of his left boot, and examination revealed a deep stab in the side of the calf. Also, as was usual for a man who had fought for any length of time in plate, the skin surfaces of his muscular body from shoulders to knees were one vast bruise, while his clothing dripped of sweat.

Vaskos's gentle probing had early established that Ahndee's left radius was broken. It was a clean break, however, and had been more or less immobilized by the tight-fitting armguard which had encased it. The broken arm did not disturb the *Keeleeohstos* and his orderly. What did was not visible until more armor was stripped off. Both the left elbow and shoulder had been sprung from their sockets! So employing rough-and-ready battlefield expedients between them, the officer and the soldier snapped the two joints back into place, then set and splintered the forearm.

Poor Ahndee recovered brief, screaming consciousness, but quickly and mercifully lapsed back into insensibility.

Upon *Komees* Djeen's return, it was decided that since a physician was known to be in residence to attend the ailing *Thoheeks,* the wounded men would be borne to Morguhn Hall, guarded by him and his troopers, while the remainder of the party returned to Horse Hall with the captured weapons, gear, and horses, most of which Hari recognized as his anyway. The broken, bloody corpses would be fetched in after sunrise.

None of *Komees* Djeen's faithful Freefighters made mention of the armored man they had found wandering the forest in a daze, nor did the old Strahteegos for he had recognized his prisoner as *Komees* Hari's valet, Kreestofohros.

It was a long, slow journey, for horse litters could not move so rapidly as riders. Dawn was paling the sky ere the van pounded their saberpommels on the thick, barred gates of Morguhn Hall.

At about the same time, in the town of Morguhnpolis, another nobleman was hearing the report of a spikebearded visitor. The visitor knelt before the lord, still in his hacked and dented armor, a bloodcrusty rag wrapped around his head and another around his right hand.

When he had mumbled the last word of his summary, the nobleman hissed, "You clumsy, witless, bungling fool!"

Jerkily, the armored man crawled a few feet closer and, raising his hands in supplication, stuttered, "Please . . . if it please my Lord . . . we did all that mortal flesh . . ."

A chopping motion of the nobleman's head silenced the supplicant. Leaning far back in his chair, he jerked a dark red rose from a silver vase on the table beside him and pressed it to his nostrils, snarling around the stem, "Get away, you pig! *Your* mortal flesh stinks, and nothing you have done or countenanced this cursed night pleases me!

"What made you think we wanted the *Thoheek*'s son killed, you witless ape? Who gave you leave to think, anyway? Better, far better, for you had you heeded the good Lady's advice!"

"But . . . but, the men . . ." the spikebearded one started.

"Damn you!" growled the nobleman. "You were represented to me as a veteran soldier, who had command experience. If you truly commanded soldiers, why can you not handle a pack of oafish servants and stupid peasants and city gutterscum? Never mind. I don't wish to hear any more of your excuses. You answer my questions, no more!

"Succinctly, then, thanks to your ill-conceived and amateurishly staged little skirmish, the *Staheerforeeah* has at least twelve members dead and as many more missing or unaccounted for, not to mention the losses of painfully collected arms and equipment. And what did this blood sacrifice buy our Holy Cause? Hah! Two barbarian mercenaries and possibly a traveling bard slain; and two nobles wounded! And one of these nobles is a *Kath'ahrohs,* to all intents and purposes, whom we still have reason to think we can convert to the True Faith. As for the other . . . what in God's name did you dimwits expect to accomplish in the death of *Thoheek*'s son, Bili?"

Eagerly, the soldier grasped at this straw which might possibly redeem him. "It has worked very well, Lord, in other places. Slay the heir and you put question to the lawful succession, and . . ."

The nobleman's fleshy lips curled back to expose his even teeth—amazingly white for a man of his middle years. "You ambulatory dungheap! This is *not* 'other places'!" he snarled. "True, the present *Thoheeks* is in ill health and, I have been reliably informed, is partially paralyzed and assuredly dying, though slowly. But—and of this matter you might have inquired before you did the irrevocable, the Lady could have told you every bit as easily as I—the death of Bili would lawfully throw the succession to Djehf, his junior by about six months. The death of Djehf would lawfully make *Thoheeks* of Tchahrlee, Bili's younger by roughly a year. The death of Tchahrlee would see the accession of Gilbuht, and the death of Gilbuht would give the title to Djaikuhb; and so on. Dammit, the *Thoheeks* has *nine* living sons! How many do you think the *Staheerforeeah* could assassinate, ere we all had a Confederation expeditionary force breathing down our necks, eh? You and those fools you presumably lead may have suicidal tendencies, but I, for one, have no wish to adorn a damned cross!

"Not only have you wasted good men on a fool's errand, but this bit of stupidity may well have jeopardized the entire structure of the *Staheerforees* in this duchy, especially if any of those missing have been taken alive!"

"But . . . but, My Lord," stuttered Spikebeard. "None of . . . they are *all* . . . all have taken the Sacred Oaths, they would never betray . . ."

The noble leaned forward and hissed scornfully. "Have you never heard of torture, then? Oaths, sacred or otherwise, mean nothing to a man whose pain is sufficiently unbearable! Oh, damn you to the lowest reaches. If they have one of ours we may have to strike ere our time is truly ripe, ere our western brothers have done their own work and can join us!"

Spikebeard raised his bloody head, squared his shoulders, fanaticism gleaming from his eyes. "Nonetheless, My Lord, you must know that we will triumph, for God, the one True God, is on our side!"

The noble sighed. "Oh, yes, we'll triumph. But lacking surprise, truly overwhelming forces, and more professionals than this Duchy can presently count, the butcher's bill will be high, very high. One look at your sorry state would tell anyone that!

"Speaking of which, one would hope that you came into the city unseen? Did you scale the wall, come through our tunnel?"

The kneeling soldier crimsoned and fidgeted. Through trembling lips, he at last managed to mumble. "I . . . I rode through the . . . the gate, My Lord. But . . . but I . . . I had my cloak so arranged that . . . that none could possibly have *seen* my armor and . . ."

The noble clenched his fists and his dark eyes flashed fire. "What in hell kind of soldier are you, or were you ever really a soldier at all? Don't you think the mercenaries at the east gate could tell you were wearing armor, cloak or no cloak, you idiot? A man carries his body differently in armor, any fool knows that!

"So you rode through the east gate, bleeding, in armor, and wearing a sword, and, fool that you are, you came directly to *my* house, eh? Damn your eyes, I should have your life . . . *would*, were you not so highly connected elsewhere!"

The kneeling man's face had faded from crimson to pasty white, his lord's reputation for cruelty being well known and equally well earned. He opened his mouth to speak, but closed it with a snap when the noble added, "And still may, if I hear one more odious yap from your dog's mouth!"

He struck a small gong on the table at his side. Two brawny, olive-skinned guards opened the door and entered, bowing.

Vahrohnos Myros waved a graceful, manicured hand at

Spikebeard. "Take him to your barracks and strip off his armor, every scrap of it, mind you. You, Ahngehlos, bundle them well, I want no one to suspect what you're carrying. Bear the armor to Paulos, the smith. Tell him to immediately break up the plates, burn off the leather, and dip the metal in acid, before he scatters it throughout his scrap heap.

"As for Captain Manos here, humm. Feelos, send a man for a physician to tend a man injured in a barracks brawl. By the time the doctor arrives, I will expect his patient to look the part. Take him away!"

CHAPTER VII

Mahrnee and Behrnees Morguhn, wrapped warmly against the chill morning air, received *Komees* Djeen and Bard Klairuhnz in the broad foyer of Morguhn Hall. Standing on the main staircase, the ladies were flanked by *Vahrohnos* Spiros Morguhn and Clanbard Hail Morguhn.

The trim old warrior marched in, his braided grey hair coiled about the crown of his head to pad the helmet he now bore in the crook of his left arm. He halted and stiffly bowed, his armor clanking.

"Ladies Morguhn, Cousin Spiros, Cousin Hail, greet the Sun. I am sorry to rouse your hall at so early an hour, but midnight last saw a brisk little melee at the Forest Bridge. I've brought a son of this House and another nobleman, both of whom are in urgent need of a physician's care."

The two women paled, but otherwise did credit to their stern upbringing.

Vahrohnos Spiros asked in a tight voice, "Be candid, Djeen. How bad are Bili's wounds?"

A smile flitted across the *Komees*'s thin lips. "Ladies and Kinsmen, we may all be proud of the lad, according to Bard Klairuhnz here. You do not know him, of course, but he is a clanless Kinsman who took part in the action, until his horse was slain and he was rendered senseless.

"He states unequivocally that our Chief-to-be fought like a treecat! Indeed, Bili captained the defense.

"Our boy has suffered a nasty split of his scalp and a

deep stab in his leg, but he's now fully awake, obviously experiencing pain, and hungry as a wolf, so I doubt me not that he'll live."

A note of sadness then entered the old man's voice. "The other nobleman is *Vahrohneeskos* Ahndros. Ahndee is not really conscious and he frequently raves in delirium."

At *Komees* Djeen's insistence, Master Ahlee saw first to Ahndee. After cursory examination, the physician and his apprentice firmly but courteously ushered all, even Mother Mahrnee, out into the corridor. When at some length he allowed them to reenter, Ahndee appeared to be sleeping peacefully and his color showed a marked improvement.

All this gave Bili time to prepare. With the aid of Mother Behrnees and a few servants, he removed his bloody, sweatsmelly clothing, bathed and donned an old, soft lounging tunic. His experience with the practice of the physician's arts had been in the Middle Kingdoms, whose nobles saw scant need to put good gold, which could be better invested in arms, armor, and condottas, into the bottomless pockets of foreigners. Therefore, although he was ravenously hungry, he refrained from eating.

When the two strangely garbed men entered his chamber, he sat on his bed, propped against a mound of pillows and taking long draughts from a leetrah-flagon of wine and brandy, steeling himself to endure the inevitable, and hoping that his body would not betray his honor—that he would neither scream nor befoul himself when the whitehot iron was pressed into his flesh.

He found the physician impressive, though he did not immediately recognize why. His height was average and Bili would have estimated his weight at perhaps eighty Ehleen keelohs, though his loose, flowing garments could easily have concealed a bulkier body. But Bili did not think this the case, for there was little surplus flesh on the dusky face and his hands were fineboned.

The master and his apprentice were dressed almost identically—loosesleeved, anklelength white robe; sleeveless, kneelength jerkin of softwoven, pale blue cotton; and well-made boots, plain ones on the feet of the apprentice, richly tooled ones on the master. The shaven scalps of both men reflected the lamplight, that of the master furrowed with old scars.

The master physician literally radiated a calm dignity and Bili found himself addressing him as an equal. "Greet the Sun, Lord Ahlee. It is not my wish to try to teach the horse how to eat grass, but I am no longer bleeding much and my pain is bearable, so tend you first to the noble Ahndee. When his hurts are eased, come you then to me."

The physician's voice was deep, rolling, and melodious. "Peace be with you, Lord Bili. We are but come from Lord Ahndee, where we corrected the well-meant damages wrought by those who first treated him. He now sleeps peacefully."

Bili nodded, set down his flagon, and turned to Mother Behrnees. "Please leave us now, Mother."

Behrnees opened her mouth to protest, but a deep look into those blue eyes—so like her loved father's—stilled her voice. And she wanted to cry, to shed tears to mourn the passing of the child and to rejoice the now obvious presence of the man.

"Please, Mother, you must go," Bili insisted in firm tones. "I know what must now be done, for I have suffered it before. And a wound burning is no place for a lady."

As Behrnees departed through the door held open by the apprentice, she thought that her heart would burst of her pride.

When his mother had gone, Bili offered a grim smile. "I await your pleasure, sir." Dubiously, he eyed the two leatherbound chests which the apprentice was opening. "Where is your brazier?"

Master Ahlee seated himself on the edge of Bili's bed and smiled. "I shall close your wounds in due time, Lord Bili, never fear. But first, tell me how you received these hurts and what varieties of weapons inflicted them."

Bili raised a hand to tap at the fresh cloths which Mother Behrnees had wound about his head. "The head wound is not much. My helm was struck and dented and the scalp beneath it split. I was struck from behind, so *I* can't say what kind of missile hit me. But I've suffered such injuries many times ere this. You have too, I'd imagine." He smiled, waving at the scars on Master Ahlee's own head.

The physician smiled also, saying softly, "No, I am no stranger to the sight of my own blood, Lord Bili. But to continue, did you swoon at the time of the injury or at any time since? Did you become dizzy or queasy? Did your vision blur? Did you feel a heaviness or a prickling in your arms and legs?"

Bili shrugged. "At the time I took the blow, it was all I could do to sit my horse, nor do I know for how long it was so. I could hear, but I could not move or speak or even open my eyes. But eventually I came back into control of myself, and then Ahndee, Mahvros, and I fought until both Ahndee and Mahvros were wounded. Then . . ."

"Wait a moment, please, Lord Bili." The physician looked puzzled. "I was not told of a *third* casualty. This man, Mahvros, did he return with your party? Do you know how serious is his wound?"

Blankfaced, Bili said, "Yes, Lord Ahlee, Mahvros was beside me for most of the journey. As concerns his wound, he took a javelin in his right shoulder. One of *Komees* Djeen's troopers is tending him down in the stables."

"Lord Bili," Master Ahlee spoke urgently, "this Mahvros must be removed from the stable as quickly as possible. There are many guest chambers in this hall. Can he not be accommodated in one?"

"No," said Bili flatly. "His kind are not allowed inside the hall."

Master Ahlee's manner cooled noticeably. "If this Mahvros was good enough to fight beside you, surely he deserves better lodgement than a stable! You disappoint me, young sir."

Bili kept his face blank with great effort. "Where else, Lord Ahlee, do the men of your own land lodge their horses?"

The physician regarded Bili's twitching mouth and mirth-filled eyes for a long moment, then grinned broadly, chuckling, "When I am done with you, Lord Bili, I shall be happy to take a look at Mahvros . . . in the stable."

Bili sobered. "Now that is most gracious of you, Lord Ahlee. I would much appreciate such generosity, for Mahvros and I are . . . well, we're closer than you probably could understand."

The physician nodded. "But I do understand, Lord Bili, and I will certainly see to your friend. Now, back to you. Have you lost consciousness or control since that first time?"

"Only once," answered Bili. "I unseated a man, threw him off his horse into the stream. But when I mounted his horse, I became very dizzy and couldn't lift my axe. Then I fell off the horse and I recall nothing more until I awakened in a horse litter."

Ahlee nodded, then shifted his position and pointed at the bandaged leg. "And how was that wound inflicted, Lord Bili?"

"I don't know," Bili admitted. "Honestly, you know how things are in battle. I can't remember even taking that wound, much less when or where or with what. From the look I got when I bathed though, I'd say a small-bladed spear or a javelin.

"But, Lord Ahlee, let me warn you. I don't think I can

remain unmoving whilst you sear these wounds. It might be better if you strapped me down, or called for servants to hold me . . . a good dozen men, anyway, for Sacred Sun has given me great strength."

Ahlee smiled again. "Yes, I am sure you are a very strong man, Lord Bili. But wait." He extended his right hand over his shoulder, palm open.

Having been busy arranging the lamps, Eeshmaheel, the apprentice, stepped back to one of the opened chests, took something from it, and laid that something in his master's pink palm.

When the physician opened his hand, Bili saw that it contained a disk of clear, smoothly polished quartz, suspended from a thin, golden chain. Ahlee held the ends of the chain, allowing the disk to dangle before Bili's eyes for a moment, then set it to spinning.

In a low, soothing, monotonous voice, he intoned, "Watch the crystal, Lord Bili. Do not take your eyes from it for a moment. Watch it, watch it, see the beauty of the light. You see? Is it not the most beautiful light you have ever seen? See the light, Lord Bili. Sink into the light . . ."

And as the voice murmured on and on, Bili found himself obeying. He sank into the light, became one with it, and it was good, that oneness was infinitely good. It was the Light of Sacred Sun and he was part of It and It was part of him, It streamed through him and of him. And from Them, worlds and universes received their substances and were born and lived countless eons and died and returned their life gift to Them. And Bili continued to sink, faster and faster and faster, spiraling tightly, bodilessly, through the unbearably beautiful, wondrous light-which-was-one-with-darkness, and Sacred Wind roared in his ears. But it roared steadily and soothingly and reminded him of the sound of that voice—what voice?—and the roar gradually faded and the spiraling went on and still he sank, descending toward the tossing waves of a great, vast, dark-light ocean. Closer to those dark, lightcrested waves he came, closer and closer and closer.

Bili steeled his light-filled, bodiless body for the chill of the water, but he eased gently into it and it closed over him and there was no chill. He was enveloped in a moist, nourishing warmth, a warmth which soothed and comforted and lulled. And in the warm, caressing, darklight nothingness, everything vanished—pain, pleasure, worry, fear, pride, desire. And Bili could not bring himself to wish them back, for all of them together could not, he knew, replace one-ten-thousandth part of the exquisite beauty of his newfound but never forgotten nothingness . . .

"The young lord journeyed quickly, Master," commented Eeshmaheel.

"Both quickly and deeply," Ahlee nodded, handing back the disc. "As I oft have said, some journey more easily than others. It helps if they have no fear, Eeshmaheel, such as this young man.

"Eeshmaheel, there are noblemen and noble men, and a man need not be one to be the other. But this man is that rarity, both together. It is seldom that Ahláh grants long life to such, but, in His wisdom, He allows them to do much good within the short time that they remain amongst men.

"Now, Eeshmaheel, uncover the head and tell me of the wound."

The apprentice first peeled back the lids and minutely examined the eyes. Then he removed the bandages, starting a fresh flow of blood. Disregarding this, he tenderly probed about the wound site, then spread the edges and sponged away enough blood to allow him a glimpse of the depths of the injury.

"Master, there is no blood on the eyes and the pupils are of equal size, nor did the patient have difficulty in focusing them before he journeyed. The swelling around the opening is hard and the bleeding had entirely ceased, ere my examination started it afresh. There is no bone visible, nor is the scalp torn, only cleanly split."

Ahlee asked, "Were you the master, what would you do?"

Eeshmaheel's brown eyes never left the wound while he answered. "Master, it has bled copiously, so is certainly cleaned of foreign matter and dirtinesses; nor is there sufficient depth for matter to hide. Since he is a cleanly man, the scalp need not be shaved. I would but place over it a thick cloth well soaked in brandy and tightly bandage it."

Ahlee raised his brows. "You would not, then, suture it? Why not?"

"Master, Ahláh already has begun to heal this wound, so it were impiety to attempt improvement upon His work. But even were the injury fresh, it is very shallow and not quite so long as my thumb. I would do no more than I have said, Master."

Ahlee nodded his approval and ordered, "Then do it, and Ahláh guide your hands." While he watched the sure, quick actions of the apprentice, he thought that very soon now Eeshmaheel would be departing, taking ship to the north. He would bear with him Master Ahlee's letter to the Elder Masters of Kohoz, to whom he would swear his oaths and begin to train his first apprentice. And the Elder Masters would send Ahlee another gangling lad.

When Eeshmaheel had done, he and the Master gently turned the patient facedown on the bed. Ahlee watched while his apprentice removed the bandage from the leg. Removal brought on no such crimson flood as had the lifting of the head bandage. There was but a continuation of the slow, steady ooze and trickle of pale-pinkish water.

"Eeshmaheel . . . ?"

The young physician—young being a relative term, for he was a good ten years older than Bili—scrutinized the wound, leaned close to sniff it, moistened a fingertip in the discharge, touched it lightly to his tonguetip, then gently kneaded the flesh about it.

"Master, it appears a deep stab, I would say at least a fingerlength. Almost did it pierce through, for the flesh opposite shows much discoloration. I would agree with the patient about the weapon involved, for a sword or dirk would have cut cleanly, but here there is some evidence of tearing. The spear was probably not poisoned though, for I can neither smell nor taste any venom. But it should have commenced to close by this time, unless those who washed him damaged it."

"Very good, Eeshmaheel, very good, all save the last. Bring the surgical chest and the brandy and I will show you why the wound continued to weep."

The apprentice never ceased to marvel at the master and had long since despaired of ever being his equal, in any save the simplest ways. Wordlessly, he poured brandy into a shallow pan, then immersed those instruments indicated by the master in the liquid. That done, he poured a generous quantity of the brandy over the master's hands, then his own.

A brief but knowing glance at the pile of clothing as he entered had provided Master Ahlee the answer to the weeping wound. Within a few, short minutes, that answer was clamped betwixt the jaws of a bloodsmeared brass forceps.

"What is it, Eeshmaheel?" He opened the instrument, dropping the gory morsel into the younger man's palm.

"Why, it is a bit of fine leather, Master. But you knew, even before you extracted it, didn't you?"

Extending his bloody hands, that the apprentice might pour over them more brandy, Ahlee admonished, "Observe, Eeshmaheel, observe! A good physician prides himself upon missing nothing. Look at that boot atop the pile near to the door. See the place where the point tore through? There is a piece missing, yes? Now, true, it could be inside the boot, or lying in the horse litter or somewhere on the road, or even back at the battleground.

But combine the two details, Eeshmaheel, a stab which will not close and a missing bit of boot."

When Bili opened his eyes, the physician still sat before him, but he no longer held the disk pendant.

He moved his leg slightly, then grimaced. "There is now a fierce stinging in both my wounds, Lord Ahlee. Perhaps your apprentice had best fetch your brazier and irons and get on with this unpleasant business. But give me a good burn on the first try, please. It's not the sort of thing I want a second serving of."

"There will be no burning of your flesh, Lord Bili," Ahlee softly boomed, smiling. "Your wounds have both been tended. The scalp will close of itself, if you are considerate of it. I have cleaned out the stab and closed it with stitches which I will remove in a week or so, Ahlâh willing. The stinging is caused partially by the stitches and partially by the reaction of the raw flesh to the brandy with which the innermost bandages are soaked. It is uncomfortable, true, but it has been observed that wounds heal more easily and quickly when such bandages are employed."

Bili's skin crawled, his neck hairs prickling. "Are . . . are you then a . . . a *sorcerer,* Lord Ahlee, to have accomplished so much in but the twinkling of an eye?"

Again, the warm, comforting smile. "Some might call certain of my skills sorcery, Lord Bili, especially my manner of willing you to sleep. But sleep you did, feeling nought of the pain of my surgery. It was barely dawning when first I came to you. The sun is now above two hours in the sky."

CHAPTER VIII

At a little past the nooning, *Komees* Djeen, *Vahrohnos* Spiros, and a half dozen Freefighters had been laboriously interrogating the luckless Kreestofohros for some hours. They had had no trouble in finding a secluded place to conduct their messy business, for Morguhn Hall was far larger than most halls and its cellars were extensive and multileveled.

Equipment and instruments were another matter, however, for their morn's labor was an activity seldom practiced in the Duchy of Morguhn, in recent years at least. On the rare occasions that *Thoheeks* Hwahruhn had ordered such, the activity had invariably been conducted at the prison in Morguhnpolis, where a qualified professional torturer-executioner maintained a modest shop. But since *Komees* Djeen wished to conceal his possession of this prisoner, use of the professional or any of his tools was out of the question. Therefore, they had had to improvise.

Thanks to hearty applications of these improvisations, Kreestofohros would never again be whole or hale or handsome. Thus far, however, all that they had wrung from his shredded lips had been screams and moans, pleas and prayers, curses. Now he had again fainted, and the troopers were finding it harder to revive him this time.

Spiros shook his head, frowning. "I like it not, Djeen."

"What else can we do?" expostulated the old Strahteegos. "*I* know there's a conspiracy and *you* know there's a conspiracy, and it's certain sure that Boy-lover Myros and that old gasbag, Skiros, are in it up to their dirty ears. But they're too big to legally touch, without proof."

"Now, I've known Hari and Drehkos all their lives and I don't like to think that one or both is into this sorry cesspool of superstition and anarchy, but . . . I told you how all his servants mysteriously disappeared last night. Well, among the scum who attacked the boys, I recognized at least four bodies. They were all Hari's people. One, who bore the mark of young Bili's big axe, was majordomo of Horse Hall!"

Spiros's eyebrows shot up. "*Hofos,* Djeen?"

"None other," growled the *Komees.* "So it becomes obvious that we have a more serious problem than we thought. If supposedly respectable upper servants of the water of Hofos and this bastard are involved, no one of the Kindred is safe in either city or country! This is another reason why we must know names, Spiros! Getting some answers from the tough nut over there is of utmost importance."

"Admitted, Djeen, admitted," Spiros nodded briskly. "And that's why I so dislike what we're doing. We are trying to perform something that we know very little about. If we're not extremely careful, we're going to take it too far and kill the prisoner. Then where will we be? Who will then give us answers or names, eh?"

Komees Djeen's roar filled the large chamber. "*Sacred Wind take it!* What else can we do?" he repeated in exasperation. "Even if we could get him into Morguhnpolis and into the prison unrecognized, how do we know that we could trust Master Mahrios? After all, if he's not a *Kath'ahrohs,* he's damned close to it!"

"Let us send for that physician, Master Ahlee," suggested the Vahrohnos. "Allow him to examine the man before we go on. And let us keep him by, that he may keep the Ehleen dog alive until we've broken him."

The trooper sent abovestairs returned with Master Ahlee's flat refusal to take any part in the proceedings, so

Vahrohnos Spiros betook himself to the suite occupied by the physician and his retinue. He was greeted courteously; but as soon as he had indicated his errand and uttered his urgent request, the friendly, brown face became devoid of expression and the tone of the deep voice took on the hardness of steel.

"My Lord Baron, I cannot condone torture. It is a bestial practice, whatever the motives of those who employ it. I have never and will never take any role in its commission! Do I make myself clear?"

"I did but request, Physician," grated Spiros, unaccustomed to noncooperation on the parts of persons of inferior rank and status. "This matter is of the gravest importance to the good of the Duchy, and too many lives may well hinge upon the information which this stubborn man can give us to cater to your likes and dislikes and whims. Therefore, I, Spiros, by grace of Sun and Wind, *Vahrohnos* of Taheerospolis and Subchief of Morguhn, do *command* your instant obedience to my wishes! Do *I* make *myself* clear, Physician?"

Ahlee drew himself up, squaring his shoulders and setting his jaw. "Perfectly clear, My Lord Baron, you speak your language well. A pity that you cannot understand it so well. But, I will repeat: *I—will—not—be—a—party—to—torture!*"

Snarling, Spiros loosened his heavy dirk. "Why you impudent barbarian pig! How dare you to disobey my order? Are you then mad? Know you not how quickly I can have your hairless head on a spear?"

Bard Klairuhnz opened the door and strolled into the chamber. With no preamble, he inquired, "Kinsman, are you then unaware that Master Ahlee, like all members of his guild within the boundaries of the Confederation, practices under the auspices and personal protection of the Undying High-Lord, Milo? It were senseless to threaten him, and it would be treasonable to harm him."

To protect the *Vahrohmos*'s pride, he had employed mindspeak.

"Kinsman," Spiros answered him silently. "You are unaware yourself, unaware of the extreme gravity of this case. *Komees* Djeen has told me much of you, and so I know that you fought hard and well to aid my House. For that reason, I'll trust you. Know you the problem." So saying he lowered his mindshield, baring the inmost recesses to Klairuhnz, that he might fully realize what had occurred and was presently occurring in the Duchy and thus better comprehend the dilemma.

And what Bard Klairuhnz learned was serious enough! The attack on Bili's party had not been the first such. Indeed, no less than three poorly armed or virtually unarmed parties of Kindred had been butchered to the last person on the roads. Within the cities, most Kindred went armed and guarded by day and by night, in justified fear of the dagger or the strangling cord. Servants of Ehleen blood were become, with few exceptions, surly and secretive, while Ehleenoee peasants and free-farmers and tradesmen were proving ever harder to deal with. And these troubles were not something which had gradually built to the present intensity, but had sprung up full-grown, just after the Duchy's last harvest.

"All right, Kinsman Spiros," Klairuhnz beamed. "I was not aware that matters had progressed so far here. And I agree that you needs must have Master Ahlee's aid. Your reasoning on that is quite sound. But he is a strongwilled man and quite stubborn on what he considers a matter of principle. Because of his protected status, you cannot physically force him to help you, and circumstances have rendered your patience too short to allow for diplomacy.

"So, it might be best, Kinsman, if you left the chamber and allowed me to attempt to reason with the physician."

"Do you think you can truly bring him around, Kinsman?" Spiros, recognizing hard truth, would now grasp at any straw.

"I think so," the Bard assured him.

Wordless, Spiros bowed stiffly toward the foreigner, nodded at Klairuhnz, spun on his heel, and stalked out.

Klairuhnz waited until the footfalls had faded into the distance, then mindspoke Master Ahlee. "You received both my mindspeak and his, then?"

Ahlee's sudden start would have been imperceptible to one not watching for it. Just as quickly as he had reacted, however, he regained his composure, then frowned, saying, "Sir, I did not bid you enter. Nonetheless, I bid you welcome and peace. What matter brings you to this humble instrument of Ahláh?"

Throwing back his head, Klairuhnz gusted a laugh at the ceiling, then went on, still in mindspeak, "Master Humble Instrument, we are both of us too old to play games and there is no time to dissemble. Your mindspeak is known to be excellent and your receptivity even better. So states the Undying Lady Aldora, and she is never wrong about such talents!"

When it came, Ahlee's mindspeak proved to be almost as strong as the Bard's own. "*Who are you?*"

Having consumed the second evening meal since the bridge fight, the Kindred nobles all gathered in Bili's spacious bedchamber. Only a few hours earlier had word reached them that Bili's only uncle, Tahneest Bili of Morguhn, had been murdered, along with his wife, two sons, and bodyguards, while journeying to Morguhn Hall. This was a grim-faced aggregation.

Bili sat propped on his greatbed, flanked on the one side by his mothers and on the other by his six-months-younger brother Djehf, who had ridden in unexpected and unannounced to spend a few weeks before the commencement of the spring campaigning in the Middle Kingdoms.

Komees Djeen had drawn a chair close to the hearth and its fire, kindled to dispel the chill of the damp, foggy night, where he sat frowning and ceaselessly cracking his big, scarred knuckles, his stiff leg extended before the blaze. Ever and again, his eye strayed to the portable bed, on which lay Ahndee's unconscious form.

Master Ahlee had permitted his patient to be borne to the conference only on condition that he remain in attendance throughout, promising to awaken the young *Vahrohneeskos* briefly, if need be. The physician sat at the head of the cot, conversing in low tones with Spiros and the Bard. Clanbard Hail leaned over the back of Spiros's chair, listening but making no comment.

Geros, clad in a new scaleshirt and abbreviated helm, occupied a low stool at his master's side. He was nervously fingering the hilt of a fine saber and hoping that he looked as hard and businesslike as the two Freefighters occupying the bench which blocked the barred door.

Two more Freefighters guarded the door of the *Thoheeks,* who had taken a turn for the worse, while Eeshmaheel and Master Ahlee's two servants, all armed, kept watch within.

All horses had been summoned from the pasture to stamp and snort in the crowded hall stables, while as much livestock as possible had been crowded into makeshift pens in the outer courtyard. Forgefire flared where the resident smith and his helpers labored, fashioning old tools and stray scraps of metal into arrowheads and points for dart and javelin, repairing plate from the armory, and straightening scytheblades. The heavy gate was barred and the iron grille which protected it from rams had been lowered into place, for the first time in any man's memory. A weaponsmaster supervised several Freefighters and servants as they assembled a pair of small catapults and a large dart thrower. The remainder of the hall's Freefighters, those of *Komees* Djeen and a number of armed servants, stood the walls.

A knock on the door of Bili's chamber brought Geros and the other two guards to their feet, hands on swordhilts. When the bench was shifted and the bar removed, the knocker was discovered to be Sami Kahtuhr, majordomo of Morguhn Hall, and now castellan as well. He was an old soldier, and his new role was quite as comfortable as the infantryman's armor he had donned.

Though grey thickly streaked his light brown hair and his face was seamed and wrinkled, he had miraculously regained a youthful appearance since *Komees* Djeen had had Morguhn Hall put on a war footing and all had begun to prepare for siege and battle. The little man probably had more Kindred blood flowing in his veins than most in the room, and he looked it—slight but wiry frame, flat muscles, fair skin, flashing blue green eyes. As a cadet of Clan Kahtuhr, he was ranked as a petty nobleman, his senior-servant status notwithstanding.

He marched over to stand between *Komees* Djeen and Bili. Although he rendered his Confederation Army salute to the younger, he rendered his report to the elder.

"My Lord, within the hour the hall will be as ready as it can be for whatever is to transpire. In addition to the noble Kindred, fifty-seven men are available. Of these, forty-five are either Freefighters or former soldiers, and the others are good men who will stand firm for the honor of Morguhn. All prisoners have been so lodged that no guard will be required, so all may man the walls if it comes to that. There is more than ample food in the magazines and near tenscore head of cattle and goats, along with threescore sheep in the main court. The numbers of fowl I know not, but they swarm near everywhere one looks, indoors and out.

"I have set those loyal servants not under arms to drawing water from the spring and the wells to fill all the cisterns. When they are done, they will set about tearing down the storage sheds outside the walls and carting the lumber within—the nearer fences as well—that we shall not lack for fuel.

"The only severe shortage will be grain and hay for the animals and the horse brothers and sisters. I sent a man to fetch back any forage that might be in Hohryos Morguhn, but he has not yet returned."

Komees Djeen's head bobbed a curt nod. "Very well, *Feelahks,* you have done well. I can but wish we had more fighters. It's a far stretch of wall for fifty-seven men and six noble Kindred to cover."

"*Six* noble Kindred?" Bili suddenly yelped. "What about me? If you think, Kinsman Djeen, that you're going to deny *me* a share of the battle, just because of a bump on my head and a nick in my leg . . ."

Mother Mahrnee's hand over his mouth muffled the rest. "Of course Bili will fight. And both my sister and I are adept with sling and huntingbow; nor are our boarspears partial to only the blood of beasts."

"Unless this be a private war," Master Ahlee said gravely, "you may include a physician who once was a warrior in your tally. Still can I cast an accurate spear, nor am I inexperienced in matters of the sword."

Komees Djeen grinned wolfishly. "All right, Feelahks Sami, you heard; everyone in this room will fight. You may add four more to your tallyroll." Then, a look of sadness crept over his face and he looked again at the recumbent form on the cot. "Would Sun would allow it to be five."

Dawn saw the Council party in the saddle. After a stirrup cup, they saw the gates close behind them and set out for Morguhnpolis at a brisk trot. In order that the hall might be the better manned, the party had been held to a bare minimum, every man of them armed to the teeth. Three hundred yards ahead of them, a single trooper rode point, his orders to return and warn, rather than fight, in the event of trouble.

Bili and Djehf rode in the van, Bili absorbed at trying to establish a decent rapport with the chestnut gelding who was Mahvros's temporary replacement, Djehf still a little dazed at the rapid and unexpected change in his rank and status. He knew that as soon as the present troubles were resolved, he must send a messenger to Eeree, for now he was never to return. With his father inches from death and his uncle slain, Bili was virtual *Thoheeks* and Chief, while he was automatically Tahneest. He knew not whether to laugh or weep, so he kept his mouth tightly shut.

The second pair of riders were *Komees* Djeen and *Vahrohnos* Spiros, who both rode in silence, each full of his own thoughts and worries. The third pair were Clan-bard Hail and Bard Klairuhnz. Hail's lips moved silently as he composed new verses to the "Song of Morguhn," while Klairuhnz was in mindspeak with Master Ahlee, on a mental level to which few men or women could attain.

Save for the fact that his sash now supported an exotically decorated, double-curved saber, Ahlee's outward appearance was but little changed. His flowing white robe still billowed, but now it concealed a longsleeved brigandine and a brace of wavy-bladed daggers, and his head-wrappings covered a steel skullcap.

Although he had both war training and experience, Ahlee basically disliked harming a fellow man under most circumstances. But what these people faced, unbelievers though they assuredly were, was a different and distinctly sinister thing, a true horror; and he was convinced that to aid them in their uneven struggle against such evil would be to strive for Ahláh. When again he thought upon the things—the godless, unclean, monstrous things—which his hypnotism had drawn from the mind and memory of that prisoner, he shuddered from head to foot. For spiritual solace, he began to chant holy verses.

The mercenary who rode beside him, leading a packmule, listened briefly, failed to understand the ancient tongue, but decided that a song was just the thing to help speed this almost-done and boring ride; whereupon he launched into an endless and endlessly obscene soldiers' song. Bili knew the particular ditty and took it up, anything to relieve some of the maddening tension. After some score of choruses, Djehf bawled a few original and recent verses from Eeree.

The bawdy old ballad brought fond memories to *Komees* Djeen and a broad smile to his face, and he joined in as well. Though he knew neither the song itself nor memories of it, Spiros found himself joining in the catchy, nonsensical chorus. And when others' recall failed, Clanbard Hail provided extemporaneous and topical verses.

While his physical being sang with the rest, Klairuhnz mindspoke Ahlee, saying, "These fine men cannot know or even suspect just how incredibly ancient this song really is. Nor do they realize that near twoscore generations of their ancestors have sung it."

"Did my antecedents also sing it, Lord?" queried the physician.

"Oh, yes, Ahlee," replied the Bard. "In those long-ago days, we were all one nation, speaking one language."

"Most remarkable," Ahlee commented, adding, "It is certain that I have then chosen aright, for surely you and your few peers are much loved of Ahláh, that He has vouchsafed you such long life."

The guards at the eastern gate of Morguhnpolis were Freefighters, mostly from the Middle Kingdoms. They laughed and buffeted each other in delight, as the noble lords entered the city singing a song they considered their own, and they enthusiastically added their voices to a chorus, feeling a fierce kinship with these fellow fightingmen.

Thus augmented, the last chorus roared up the all but deserted east-west thoroughfare, "*HINKEE DINKEE PAHRLEE VOOOO!*"

CHAPTER IX

Bili's party dismounted before the city palace, more than three hundred years old, dating from the period before his ancestors had crossed the mountains, when Morguhnpolis—then called Eeleeoheepolis—had been the northwestern jewel of the Crown of Karaleenos. It was an impressive building, fashioned of native granite and faced with that hauntingly beautiful greygreen limestone from Kehnooryohs Ehlahs. Its main chamber was almost as large as the outer courtyard of Morguhn Hall and was columned and paved with colored and veined marbles; but it was very difficult to heat, so was seldom used for anything. The footfalls of the noblemen echoed as they traversed the length of the huge chamber and mounted the wide marble stairs toward the second floor Council Chamber.

Komees Djeen frowned at sight of the four pikemen ranged before the tall, brass-sheathed doors of the Council's meetingroom. They were not the usual Freefighter guards, but rather civilian Spearlevymen, Ehleenoee all. A skinny corporal of the same body stood just behind the pikemen, holding his knife-edged thrusting spear as though it were a frog gig.

Eyes fixed dead ahead, Bili and Djehf clanked toward the doors, outwardly unconcerned. After nervously licking his lips, the corporal hissed a whispered order and the levymen sloppily presented their pikes, no two at the same angle. *Komees* Djeen snorted in disgust and made a decidedly uncomplimentary remark concerning gutter-scum playing at soldier.

Bili and Djehf marched forward until the glittering points were but inches from their breastplates. The brothers stood thus for a moment. Then Djehf suddenly grasped the crossbar of the pike before him and savagely jerked it from the hands of its wielder. The levyman spun half around and, ere he could turn back, Djehf dropped the captured pike and booted the man's rump so hard that he went sprawling, sliding a good way down the slick floor of the side hallway on his breastplate. Grinning, he reached for a second pike, but the levymen hastily grounded their weapons and backed up until the walls ended their retreat, leaving their corporal to guard the portals alone.

"The Council Chamber," began that worthy, in a piping falsetto squeak. He flushed, cleared his throat, presented the long, wide blade of his spear, and started over. "The Council Chamber is forbidden to any save confirmed members of the Thirds!" He spoke in Old Ehleeneekos.

Komees Djeen shouldered between Bili and Djehf, demanding, "What language are you grunting in, you puling shoat?"

Before the unhappy man could frame an answer, Djehf's powerful hand had closed on the shaft of the short spear. In a brittle voice, he announced, "If you don't let go of that piece of junk, dungface, by Sun and Wind, I'll bugger you with it!"

The corporal did let go, but not quickly enough to suit Djehf, who jerked the Ehleen away from the closed door, spun him about, and jabbed a good two inches of the broad spearpoint into his seat. The man screamed, then sped down the side hall, clutching at his bleeding posterior and howling like a moon-mad hound. Three pikes fell clattering and three pikemen followed their wounded leader as fast as their legs would carry them.

Jerking wide the brazen doors, the brothers stalked into the Council Chamber, the rest of their party hard on their heels.

The T-shaped Council Table filled the center of the chamber. The places of the Second and Third Thirds were ranged on either side of the shaft, while those of the First Third were along the crossbar. No one, of course, occupied the chairs of the First, but all five of the Third were filled and four of the second had occupants. A bench against the side wall held a flashy fop, a black-bearded man in the robes of a subpriest, and a beefy, balding lout in a stained butcher's apron. At each of the chamber's four corners stood a Spearlevyman with grounded pike, all obviously of near-pure Ehleen blood.

Speaking no word, glancing neither to right nor left, Bili strode to the central chair of the First Third. Before he seated himself, however, he drew his heavy broadsword and laid it near to hand, pointing it down the length of the T's shaft. He imperiously waved his brother to the chair at his right, while *Komees* Djeen moved to his accustomed place, along with Spiros and Hail. Klairuhnz leaned a hip against the end of the table, near Ahndee's empty seat. Master Ahlee had carefully closed the doors and now loitered close to them.

Bili let his gaze travel down the two rows of faces. Nearest him on either side of the board sat *Komees* Hari and Feelos Pooleeos, the merchant, and the faces of both men looked deeply troubled. Beyond Hari lounged *Vahrohnos* Myros, a mocking smile on his fleshy lips, but pure, distilled hatred beaming from the glittering black eyes which briefly locked with Bili's. Beyond him sat Drehkos, who gave Bili a nervous, uncertain smile; and *Vahrohneeskos* Stehfahnos, slender but supple looking, who stared back levelly and coolly, from eyes as blue as Bili's, despite the Ehleen's black hair.

Across from Ahndee's empty place sat *Kooreeos* Skiros, apparently oblivious to the highly charged atmosphere. He was talking softly with the wizened, beaknosed little man on his right, Nathos Evrehos, the goldsmith-moneylender. Lastly, Bili gave a hard stare to Paulos, Guildmaster of the duchy's blacksmiths, and bastard half brother of the dying *Thoheeks*. The insolent, hateful glare that he got in return set the blood to pounding in his temples. Some of his anger must have been visible, for *Komees* Djeen hastily laid a hand on Bili's armguard, then hastened to speak before Bili might.

"Why," he demanded in clipped tones, "have our well-paid Freefighters been replaced with piketoting amateurs, Myros? I'm certain sure it's your idea. Sun and Wind, man, you come up with more harebrained schemes than a full troop of village idiots could concoct! Since we're paying good gold to professional swords, why deprive the fields and streets of ploughboys and dungscoopers?"

Myros grinned. "There are less than twoscore mercenaries left, and they remain only because some fool hired them to a contract of twenty-six, rather than twenty-four moons. As fast as the barbarians' contracts expired, I have let them go. Almost all the city guards are now men who bear their arms for their homes and their lands." The *Vahrohnos*'s grin had metamorphosed into a twisted grimace. His features were empurpling with his passion and his eyes gleamed the feral fire of fanaticism. "Not for mere gold do these men bear arms, but for their Faith and their long-lost heritage!"

To Bili, it seemed obvious that his mothers had erred in their judgment of Myros's case, for the rebellious dog appeared to believe every word churned out by his sewer-mouth.

Count Djeen crashed his gauntleted fist against the tabletop, grating, "That cuts it, you boyloving dungwallower! Such abuse of your authority cannot be tolerated! You are hereby relieved as governor of this city. Depart this chamber and await Council's censure."

Myros's laugh was cold and sharp as midwinter icicles.

Lounging back in his chair, he exchanged a knowing glance with *Kooreeos* Skiros, whose teeth flashed through his thick black beard. Then the Vahrohnos stared insolently into the *Komees*'s one blue eye, drawling, "I think not, you old fool, I think not."

The elderly nobleman snapped to the nearest pikeman, "Guard, escort the *Vahrohnos* Myros from this chamber!"

The levyman only sneered. The *Kooreeos*'s smile broadened, Guildmaster Paulos smirked, and the goldsmith snickered, echoed by the three interlopers on the bench.

"He has stopped taking orders from your ilk, you heathen squatter," said Paulos, through his smirk. "We all have. This city of Eeleeoheepolis is back in the hands of its rightful owners and soon all the duchy will be!"

"This city," answered Bili, in a hard voice, "is called Morguhnpolis and is the property of Clan Morguhn, as is the Duchy. That is the established order of things. But the borders of this my Duchy are not closed, as well you know, smith! Any free man who likes not *my* overlordship has my leave to quit these lands!"

Paulos stood and leaned down the table toward Bili. "Keep barking, you arrogant young puppy, sitting in the chair which should be mine! I, Paulos Morguhn, am rightful owner of Morguhn Hall, and you are all usurpers of *my* properties and titles and . . ."

Both Myros and the *Kooreeos* snapped, "Enough, Paulos!"

But there was no stopping the raving man. White patches of froth had formed at the corners of his mouth, his face was working, and his eyes were become wide and wild. ". . . when I am in my own, you'll whine and whimper, not bark! I'll have your nuts out, damn you, I'll have the nuts of all of you what was sired by that boarhog, Hwahruhn! And I'll sell your brothers for *poosteesee*, and I'll keep you to be my own loveboy, after I get tired of plowing the butterhaired bitches what whelped you! And I'll . . ."

Bili and Hail were a fraction of a second too late in attempting to restrain Djehf. The weight of his armor notwithstanding, he leapt onto the table. In the twinkling of an eye, he was down its length and the steelshod toe of his hardswung boot had smashed Paulos's mouth to a pulpy red ruin! The Guildmaster's chunky body went back into his chair with such force that the wood cracked, splintered, collapsed, and dumped him on the floor. He lay halfconscious, moaning and making gurgling noises.

Myros jumped to his feet, drawing his sword. Waving it at Djehf, he shouted at the pikemen, "Kill the heathen!"

As the first levyman to obey stepped abreast of Master Ahlee, he abruptly voiced a keening wail and let go his pike to clutch at his left side. Ahlee pushed his victim away and, half turning, threw the bloody dagger at another pikeman. All six inches of wavy blade disappeared into that man's belly, just below his breastplate. His scream sounded unearthly.

Myros, too, screamed, at the top of his lungs. "*GUARDS! GUARDS! TO ME!*"

A multitude of feet pounded along the side corridors, but Ahlee snatched up the pike at his feet and ran the thick ash shaft through the gilded-bronze door rings. He turned back and drew his silver-hilted yataghan barely in time to counter the vicious downswing of Myros's saber. But a twist of the brown wrist all but spun the weapon from Myros's grasp and Ahlee's lightening-fast riposte would have hamstrung the *Vahrohnos,* had he not hastily hopped backward. And speedily as the Ehleen moved, his opponent's blade still managed to slice into the upper cuff of his boot, bringing blood from the flesh it covered.

Knifing the first pikeman, Bili had kicked over his chair, grasped his naked broadsword, and bounded over to cut down the closest levyman. The last pikeman did manage to reach the table, but as he made shift to jab at young Djehf, the straps of his breastplate were grabbed by *Komees* Hari, who jerked him backward while running the full length of his dress dirk between the short-ribs. Freeing his blade with a cruel twist, he snatched up the falling pike and backed to stand beside Spiros Morguhn.

The merchant, Feelos Pooleeos, hastily armed himself with the pike, sword, and helm of Bili's victim and took his place with the Kindred nobles.

Although Myros had always been accounted one of the best swordsmen of the duchy, he found himself fighting for his very life! Since his initial downswing, he had been constantly on the defensive, never having the opportunity to attack, all his skill and strength directed to keep the flickering, steel blur which was his adversary's cursive blade out of his flesh. Nor had his best efforts been entirely successful, for he showed blood in three places and was being driven back across the room.

"*Stehfahnos!*" he finally panted. "Help me!"

But Stehfahnos' sword stayed in its scabbard and Stehfahnos himself was dead on the marble floor. The youngest Morguhn left the tabletop to engage the butcher and the fop, who were trying to unbar the doors.

Cursing, the fop left the butcher to tug at the tightly wedged pikeshaft alone. Drawing a slender, ornate thrustingsword, he extended his arm to jab at the armored man's unprotected face. Djehf's powerful upswing shattered the fop's brittle weapon and his downstroke severed the swordarm, just above the wrist. The fop fell to his knees, staring in horrified fascination at his hand lying before him on the floor, slowly releasing its grip on the hilt of the broken sword.

Djehf stalked purposefully toward the butcher. Unarmed, that man backed along the wall, his hands held before him. His fear-filled eyes locked on that broad, bloody blade.

Kooreeos Skiros stood at the table, alternately calling for the guards and vainly shouting a command for all combat to cease. Klairuhnz stood close by the cleric, watching his every move. All at once, he leaned close and spoke a few words. Bili failed to hear the Bard's words, for they came at the same time as the butcher's death cries, and also because someone in the corridor had collected his wits and brought up something to use as a ram. The doors were groaning and the two-inch pikeshaft beginning to crack.

Whatever was said, it clearly startled the *Kooreeos*. His bushy black eyebrows shot up and his right hand dived under his robes, to reemerge holding what Bili assumed was a throwing club—a thick, L-shaped piece of greyish metal. Grasping one arm of it, he pointed the other at Klairuhnz's middle.

But Klairuhnz clamped both hands around the club and twisted it out of the *Kooreeos*'s hands, then slammed the side of it against its owner's temple. Skiros's boneless collapse set the subpriest to shrieking in harmony with the moneylender, who shared his haven under the table.

Shoulderblades pressed to the wall, Myros could retreat no further. He had not again been blooded, but his right arm, from shoulder to fingertips, was a tingling, fiery agony, bespeaking the force of the blows his blade had turned. He knew that he could not turn another, so he opened his trembling hand and the saber clattered to the floor.

"Mercy, please, mercy," he gasped. "Spare my life, sir, I . . . I beg you."

Hardly had the words left his lips, when the much-abused pikeshaft finally snapped and the doors burst open before a wave of pikemen. Behind them were ranged a half-dozen archers with arrows nocked; behind the archers were two Ehleenoee officers, another subpriest, and Djaimos the carter, who had arrived too late to "participate" in this Council meeting.

"Heathen barbarians," shouted the subpriest. "Surrender!"

"Yes, surrender!" echoed one of the officers. "Surrender or we'll slay you all!"

Fast as a snake, Ahlee dropped his yataghan, jerked Myros close, and gave him a good look of the wavy blade of his second dagger, before poising it at the *Vahrohnos*'s throat.

"Cowardly dog," he hissed. "As you see, this blade is envenomed. If but a single bow is drawn or one spearman advances, I shall inflict the tiniest of cuts in your flesh, following which you will die slowly and in unimaginable agony. Now, speak to your hounds!"

Drehkos flatly refused to accompany them, answering his brother's entreaties with words which staggered the master of Horse Hall. So they left him in the gory Council Chamber, along with the dead and the wounded, the disarmed soldiers and officers, the two subpriests and the moneylender, who had swooned of fright. Myros and the unconscious *Kooreeos* they took with them.

The heavy manacles, brought by one of the officers, had been intended to chain such of them as were taken alive. Now they were adapted to secure the battered doors. The Council Chamber had no windows, the visitors' bench was bolted to the floor, and the table could not have been lifted by twice the number of Ehleens present. Consequently, the Kindred hoped to be out of the city ere the prisoners could break out and spread the alarm.

The stairs seemed endless, but the little party finally reached the foot and hurried, almost at a jogtrot, through the huge, dim expanse of the main chamber. When they were nearly at the gaping entrance, they spied armored men beyond it, between them and safety. Coming to a halt, they drew their steel and formed a wedge, with Klairuhnz, Ahlee, and the two hostages at its core. Resolutely, they paced forward, out into the sunlight.

But the knot of men on the broad verandah were scaleshirted Freefighters, not levymen. A thick-limbed, broken-nosed man of middle years stepped out and approached them. His open hands held well away from his swordbelt, he respectfully addressed *Komees* Djeen.

"Lord Strahteegos, we gave our Swordoaths to you. Please release us of them, sir. Only two-and-thirty of us Freefighters remain in Morguhnpolis and . . . and, sir, the city has . . . has *changed.* We fear for our very lives. If . . . if you will release us, we'll . . . we'll just forget the back pay."

Bili had instantly recognized in the man's speech the slightly nasal accent of one who had grown up speaking the Harzburk dialect and he now bespoke him in that tongue, saying, "Two-and-thirty, you say? I see but a score of you."

"This one speaks for all, My Lord." The grizzled man answered, with a shy smile, in his native speech. "Twelve of ours are on guard at the east gate. Your . . . your pardon, My Lord, but . . . you serve King Gilbuht?" He had, of course, recognized the distinctive style of Bili's armor.

Komees Djeen answered, "He did, soldier, but no more. This is Bili, the new *Thoheeks* and Chief of Morguhn, your employer."

"How are you called, Freefighter?" snapped Bili. "And have you mounts?"

"Aye. My Lord, most of us have either a horse or a mule, though some had to be sold to keep us fed and housed and clothed, when Baron Myros there refused us our pay," replied the speaker, adding humbly, "This one is called Pawl, sir, Pawl Raikuh. Will . . . please, will My Lord absolve us of our Swordoaths?"

Bili shook his head. "Certainly not. I have need of your swords, though not as city guards. You and your men will ride with me, Captain Raikuh."

"With a right good will, My Lord, sir." Raikuh's head bobbed assent. "But, My Lord, this one is not a captain, only a common Freefighter."

"Not if you speak for over thirty men, you're not," said Bili curtly. Then he raised his voice, addressing the group of bravos. "What say you, Freefighters? You chose him to speak for you. Would you have him to command you, if he can assure you continued employment and," he added shrewdly, "your back pay?"

Almost as one, the men smiled and nodded. A much scarred little man stepped forward. "My Lord, Pawl, be noble born, and ain't none but respects him. He'll be a good captain, he will."

"Who is the man who speaks, Captain?" Bili demanded.

The new-made officer did not need to look. "Stanlee Krahndahl, My Lord, a Klahkzburker."

"Will he make a decent lieutenant for your condotta, Captain?"

"Indeed yes, Duke Bili!"

"So be it, then." Bili strode off toward the horses, adding, "Get your men in the saddle, all of them. And bring along spare horses for your men at the gate, plus a few more. I care not where or how you obtain them, Captain, just get them. After all, I own everything in this city, if I choose to lay claim to it!"

"Sacred Sun!" swore Spiros, in a hushed, awed aside to Djeen as they mounted. "Young, he may be, but by Wind our Bili is a *Thoheeks* to reckon with! He's the kind of chief we've needed . . . well, since the death of his grandfather, anyway. Did you see the way that that Raikuh looked at him, when he bade him commandeer horses? I think that man'd willingly die for Bili, and he'd never seen or heard of him two minutes ago!"

The old man nodded, showing every tooth in an opposum grin. "Aye, Spiros, Bili has it all—brains, guts, weapons skill, and a rare ability to handle men, to command loyalty and respect. He'll be a good chief right enough, but wasted in that capacity all the same. What an officer he'd make for the Confederation!"

While the two troopers were getting the bound and unconscious bulk of the *Kooreeos* lashed behind his saddle, Klairuhnz listened in on Djeen's comments and found himself in heartfelt agreement.

Myros, tied facedown behind *Komees* Djeen's saddle, had recovered his breath as well as his supercilious manner. "Listen to me, *Komees* Djeen. Despite the crimes to which you were a party upstairs, if you and the others will surrender to me now, I give you my word that you'll have an impartial hearing and a quick, painless death."

Djeen snorted scornfully. "Your word, Myros? Your word pledged your loyalty to Bili and his father, when you were confirmed to your title and lands. Today has proven your precious word to not be worth a scant measure of turkey dung!"

"The House of Morguhn," snarled Myros, "is and has always been usurping squatters, old man! *My* ancestors held this land when yours were scratching fleas on the Sea of Grass! The very first King of Karaleenos . . ."

"The very last King of Karaleenos," the one-eyed *Komees* coldly interrupted, "is generations dead! You are a rebel, a traitor, a liar, a murderer, and, I doubt me not, much more and worse besides. In the Middle Kingdoms, such a one as you would be slowly whipped to death or impaled. When your mind runs to quick, painless deaths, you had best pray your obscene god for one. For do not forget, you forsworn pig, Bili's upbringing was in the Middle Kingdoms!"

"*Ha!*" exclaimed Myros. "Dream on, dream on. You barbarians will never leave my city alive! You . . . *gaaaagh!*"

He broke off in a strangled scream, as the *Komees* sunk the needle point of his hook deep into the prisoner's thigh. As he jerked out the brass hook, he grimly admonished, "Another word out of you, overassumptive degenerate, and I'll jam my hook up your arse, and don't think I won't!"

But it began to appear that Myros might have been correct, for a growing rabble of Morguhnpolisee were beginning to mill about the foot of the formal garden which fronted the city palace. Few were armed at all and most of those ill armed, though more than a few pikepoints glittered above them. However, there were already several hundred there being harangued by priests, and the side streets and alleys were debouching more.

Slapping down his half visor, Bili uncased his axe, wishing for the umpteenth time that it was reliable Mahvros he bestrode, rather than this green, less than intelligent gelding. The others ranged out on his flanks, most now bearing one of the twelve-foot pikes, as well as the swords and light axes they had brought into the city.

Djehf hefted the heavy shaft, eyeing the wicked, two-foot blade. "I've never before used one of these for a lance, Lord Brother, and it's not really weighted properly for that purpose, but," he chuckled, "I trow I'll spit me a few, fat Ehleenoee ganders on it!"

Bili nodded shortly. "Aye, we must make do with the weapons to hand. Be sure that you ride well clear of me, youngster. I'd hate to axe you in error."

Djehf laughed merrily. "Never you fear, Lord Brother, I've ridden the battle line with axemen, ere this. Besides, I've an odd aversion to being axed—in error or otherwise."

Toeing his gelding forward of the line, Bili reined him about and visually inspected his minuscule force. Klairuhnz, having had second thoughts, had transferred *Kooreeos* Skiros's limp body to the withers, where he could more easily keep an eye on him. As Bili watched, the Bard drew the saber that had served so well at the bridge fight and the sunlight flashed along its polished blade. Master Ahlee, like Djehf, bore a pike, as did all the others save for *Komees* Djeen. His troopers had helped him replace his hook with another, larger one with a cleaverlike blade welded to its flat side, while his one hand held his military broadsword. Most of the baggage had been unceremoniously dumped, that Feelos Pooleeos —wearing a too small cuirass and an infantry helm— might be mounted on the sumpter mule.

The *Thoheeks*'s oldest son addressed them soberly. "We must strive to remain together, but any man who *is* separated must fight free as best he can. Against so many, all must depend upon shock and speed. If we halt for any reason, we are lost. We . . ."

But *Komees* Djeen interrupted him, pointing with his sword at something behind the young leader. "Bili . . . look you yonder."

Struck as much by the old nobleman's paling face as by the tightness of his voice, Bili reined around to gaze in the direction indicated. A knot of armored horsemen had crested the next slope of the hilly city and were extending lines to completely block the street behind the mob. Nothing about their appearance was clear; they were just black figures against the blaze of the morning sun; but there seemed a goodly number of them, at least three times the number of Bili's party.

"Well," the young axeman remarked to no one in particular, "I suppose this is as good a place to die as any."

CHAPTER X

When first Lord Myros had appointed him Warder of the East, Hahrteeos Kahrahmahnlees had had carpenters and stonemasons make certain alterations in the two rooms which were the second and third levels of the gate tower, where he would have to spend so much time. Then he had brought from his family mansion the furniture and appointments to allow him to, in his words, "live as an Ehleen gentleman should." The sparsely furnished, dimly lit, stonewalled chambers above and below his rooms he deemed fit only for his gaunt, ragged barbarian mercenaries.

The moment the heathen-devils had clattered in through his gate, he had dispatched his Ehleen sergeant, Toorkos, to Lord Myros, alerting the *Vahrohnos* of the imminent arrival of his victims-to-be at the city palace. Shortly thereafter, he had carefully locked his second-level sittingroom-office—well aware that the long-unpaid mercenaries were not above theft of small valuables, as he had had the pleasure of watching two of them beheaded for that very offense on a recent occasion—then repaired to his luxurious bedroom on the third level, having in mind an hour's diversion with Peeos, his well-trained catamite.

Despite the Undying High-Lord's abolishment of the institution of slavery nearly a hundred years before, some Ehleenoee still risked the ruinous fines and held one or two. Lord Drehkos was one such and Lord Myros owned an even dozen. Therefore, one of Hahrteeos's first actions after the death of his father was to journey to the port city of Sahrahspolis and buy this boy from a ship captain with whom Myros had done much business over the years.

Naturally, the bootlegger did not say where or how he had come by the lad, but it was certain that the twelve- or thirteen-year-old had seen his birth in none of the Ehleen lands, for his skin was darker even than the skins of the folk of the Black Kingdoms, and his speech, to his new master, was a totally incomprehensible babble. Hahrteeos had brought his acquisition back to Morguhnpolis and had had his servants teach it at least a smattering of Ehleeneekos. It had been Hahrteeos's personal pleasure to teach the slaveboy other things, breaking his will to resist by denial of food and application of pain.

But it seemed he had scarcely commenced his enjoyments in the tower bedchamber when several pairs of heavy feet clumped up the stairs beyond the door, then stamped thunderously about the guardroom above, their owners all the while chattering in the decidedly unlovely barbarian languages, of which Hahrteeos took pride in knowing not a word. Next, feet descended the stairs to the second level and a pounding on the door of his office ensued. Then one set of the feet reascended to the third level and knuckles rapped boomingly on his bedchamber portal.

Furious at this unwonted and unwanted invasion on his privacy, Hahrteeos pulled a tunic over his nakedness and threw open the door.

"*Well?*" he angrily demanded of the mercenary who had knocked. "What is it, you barbarian ape?"

It was Pawl Raikuh who stood before him, though this fact was unknown to Hahrteeos, who had not bothered to learn the names of any of "his" troops, other than Toorkos who was, after all, an Ehleen.

After saluting, the mercenary humbly requested permission to exchange some of the off-duty men for those presently on gate watch. Hahrteeos snorted his leave and, promising dire doom to the next man who saw fit to disturb him, slammed the door.

But less than a quarter hour later, another pair of feet sped up the steps. This time it sounded as if someone were attempting to split the door with a battleaxe! Hahrteeos was in a towering rage when he opened the door.

But this caller was not a mercenary. He was, rather, Stavros Klahreedees, Warder of the South and Hahrteeos's military, if not exactly social, equal, so there was nothing to do but invite him in and proffer wine. While the Warder of the East was filling his associate's goblet, more sets of big feet stomped up and past his door, but he ignored them.

The short, skinny, pockfaced visitor removed his gilded helm and laid it on a marbletopped table before he accepted, tasted, and savored a goblet of the wine. "Ahhh," he sighed. "You certainly know how to live, my dear. Would that I could afford such a home away from home, such civilized delights, such fine wines . . ."

"You will," Hahrteeos assured him, smilingly. "You will yet, once we've cleared the heathen from these lands of ours. Why, Lord Myros says . . ."

"Your pardon, please, love." The caller, with a wrinkling of his brows, set down his silver goblet. "Your pardon, but that brings me to my reason for being here. I received word, a few minutes agone, that the Lord Drehkos has commanded all gates closed immediately. That farce at the palace is done. The pigs got away from the guards by seizing and holding the Holy Skiros and Lord Myros and they must not be allowed to escape the city.

"Would you like for me to issue the necessary orders?" he asked considerately. "After all, darling, you are hardly garbed for a stroll on the walls."

Hahrteeos smiled. "How thoughtful, dear Stavros. I appreciate such kindness."

Setting his helm back on his head, Stavros turned to open the door. Taking the pullring in hand, he pulled, but the door failed to budge. Several more pulls and the addition of his other hand produced no better results. Then his bigger, heftier host took his place, but the stubborn portal failed to yield to him either.

Stavros stamped his small foot in exasperation. "What's wrong with the cursed thing? We've got to do something, you know. Those pet pigs you command are stupid enough to let the butterhaired heathens ride out of our city without a by-your-leave!"

"Patience, patience." Hahrteeos patted his guest on the shoulder. "With all of the damp weather we've had, the door or the frame has probably just developed a warp, that's all. Not that I'll not have a few larcenous carpenters well striped for it. But there is another way to reach the guardroom. Here, I'll need your help."

Between them, the two warders managed to get an old, heavy wooden ladder from behind the wall hanging which had concealed it; then wrestled it across to the center of the room, raised it, and wedged the upper tips of its uprights into ceiling grooves provided for the purpose.

Hahrteeos stepped back, breathing heavily. "These ladder and trapdoor arrangements are how they got from one level to another in the ancient days, before the outside stairway was built. See those two round holes up there? Put your fingers in them and slide the panel to the right and you'll be in the middle of the guardroom."

The boy Peeos had pulled a satin sheet over his nakedness when the caller had been admitted, turning his face to the wall and lying absolutely motionless. His master's temper was hair-triggered and terrifyingly unpredictable. The tiniest word or gesture could draw down his wrath and savage cruelties. Peeos wanted no more scars, so he took no chances. But the sounds of the raising of the ladder piqued his curiosity. He slyly turned his head and watched from beneath lowered lids.

Stavros mounted the ladder until he could reach the fingerholes and followed Hahrteeos's instructions. The long-unused panel was difficult at first, but he finally managed to get it out of the way. Then he climbed a couple of more rungs and his head, arms, and shoulders were in the guardroom.

Peeos and Hahrteeos heard him give his order; next he shouted something, then started a scream which suddenly ended in an odd gurgle. His legs commenced kicking and his arms came back into view, twitching strangely; it appeared that he was suspended by his head alone. It was so for but a brief moment, then legs and arms and body crashed down onto Hahrteeos's fine carpet, soaking it with fantastic quantities of blood.

Shrieking mindlessly, Hahrteeos dashed to the door and frantically ripped at it, heedless of the ruination of his soft hands and carefully tended nails. But the door remained closed and the Warder of the East backed into the corner, as far as he could get from that bloody, still-twitching horror at the foot of the ladder.

Pawl Raikuh came down that ladder agilely, his gory sword in hand, followed by three of his men, all four of them generously splashed with fresh blood. At his shout, the "jammed" door swung open easily and several more Freefighters trooped in. When they had drained the last of the wine from the silver ewer, they began a hot argument over to whom it now belonged, but Pawl ended it.

"Henree, bundle the ewer and the goblets into that fancy cloak yonder. Plunder will be property of all the condotta. And get the rings and armlets and all else of value off this dead pig. But don't kill that one behind the door. If I think aright, there's one here has more claim on his worthless life than do any of us."

Peeos did not fear death; indeed, only the strictest supervision by Hahrteeos and his servants had prevented the boy from taking his own life, after he came to realize for just what uses his master had purchased him. So as the huge, hard-looking soldier approached, Peeos bared his bony chest, pointed first at the naked sword, then at the area above his heart.

Captain Raikuh smiled and shook his head. "I don't mean to slay you, lad. Do you want your freedom?"

Peeos stared at the figure looming over him and shook his blue black head with its covering of tight ebon curls.

Raikuh had spoken in Mereekuhn, or the Confederation dialect of that ancient tongue; now he repeated himself in Ehleeneekos.

Hesitantly, his lips painfully shaping the words, Peeos spoke. "Free-dom? Mean when . . . no, what? Mean what, Lord Master? Peeos not under . . . not . . . ?"

Pawl whirled and strode purposefully over to the corner that held the trembling, pasty-faced Hahrteeos. Grabbing a handful of the Ehleen's perfumed hair, he dragged him to the center of the room and demanded, "What language does yonder lad speak, you sad excuse for a man?"

Hahrteeos moved his well-chewed lips, but no sounds issued from them. Pawl tried raising his sword threateningly, but his captive's only reactions were to start screaming again and to explosively befoul himself. Pawl dropped the Warder of the East disgustedly and paced back over to the bed. One after another, he tried the many languages and dialects he had learned in his nearly thirty years of Freefighting. Time was very short, and he was getting desperate, when he asked his question in Kweebehkyuhn. He nearly dropped his sword when the black-skinned boy answered him, not in that far-northern tongue, but in one which sounded much like it.

Over his shoulder, Pawl called urgently, "Frahnswah? Where is Frahnswah?"

"Here. Pawl . . . uh, Captain, I mean."

The situation was quickly explained and, in his own native tongue, Frahnswah stated, "We are leaving this city, little man. If you would leave with us and be free of your master and his *vice contre natur,* speak now."

But once the boy was clad, it was discovered that none of the spare jazerans were small enough to fit him.

Pawl declared, "There's like to be some hard fighting, an' our new lord is what he seems. The lad will be dead meat, and quickly, if . . . wait, that pig we had the head from, his is a damned small body. Let's have off his cuirass and see if that won't fit our new comrade here."

The gilded corselet proved only a little too big, while the greaved boots and the flashy helm fitted perfectly. A few more holes were punched in the swordbelt and it was buckled around the boy's waist. Pawl found the late Stavros's swordblade to be inferior and its hilt nought but gilded copper. He threw it in a corner, saying to one of his men, "Buhk, you, Henree, and Frehd take our dear commander's keys and see what's worth taking in his office, and one of you be sure to bring his small target and his shortsword for the lad."

Lastly, the Captain drew Stavros's dirk and tested its edge and point on a callused thumb, then handed it back to its new owner, commenting to his departing men, "You can at least trust these damned Ehleenee for that. Their swords may be all glitter and show, but their backstabbers will be fine steel every time!"

Hahrteeos had been lashed, hand and foot, to the sturdy uprights of the ladder, and Pawl led the armored boy over to the blubbering captive. With Frahnswah translating his words, he said, "Son, we all know of the odious bondage in which this degenerate has held you. If any man owns the right to exact the suffering and death of Lord Hahrteeos, it is you. Your dirk there is a good weapon. Use it on him in any way you wish, but whatever you do do it quickly, for we all now have horses and our new lord awaits us."

Bili shook his head sadly. They might have had a slim chance to hack through the ill-armed mob, but an uphill charge against so many mounted warriors could have but the one certain outcome.

Then, above the tumult of the rabble, came first the clatter of galloping hooves, then a swelling roar of deep voices bellowing the traditional battlecry of Freefighters:

"*BLOODBLOODBLOODBLOOD!*" It changed, as the charging horsemen neared the rear of the mob, to "*MORGUHN! DUKE BILI! MORGUHN! MORGUHN!*"

In a tight column of fours, Pawl Raikuh's veterans struck with the irresistible force of a tidal wave! The mob gave way before those flashing sabers, surging up into the lower reaches of the formal gardens, where they were met by the furious charge of Bili and the gentry. At that juncture, the mob ceased to be, dissolving into a broil of panic-stricken men and women, running, scuttling, clawing at whomever blocked their way, scurrying up sidestreets and narrow alleys, the Ehleenoee officers and priests in the van!

Komees Djeen cursed all the way back to Morguhn Hall. For in the hoorah of the charge his prisoner had either fallen or been dragged from off his horse, and they had been able to find neither hide nor hair of the traitorous *Vahrohnos*. *Kooreeos* Skiros was still captive however. He had regained consciousness and was loudly damning each and every one of them, promising dire and despicable deaths and afterlives of unspeakable torment if he was not immediately set free and returned to the city. When the subbishop's outbursts lost their amusement value, a couple of Raikuh's men helped Klairuhnz to gag his prisoner with a bloodcaked bandage rag and an old bowstring. Then they lashed him into the saddle of a spare horse, face to tail!

Poor Hari rode slumped in his saddle, world-heavy with his sorrows and suddenly appearing older than even

Djeen. It was not so much that his wife was now definitely known to be an important member of the rebellion conspiracy, for she had always despised anything which smacked of the Kindred and hated her husband for his Horseclans blood and ways. Nor was it the defection of his younger brother, for Drehkos had ever been unpredictable in his behavior and a frequent champion of questionable people and causes. That his three unmarried daughters were probably in the thing as well was of no real importance, for since they had ceased to be children, they had been but relative strangers who happened to share his hall, board, and name.

All of these smaller sorrows of course added their own less significant weights to the burden on Hari's laden soul, but what truly crushed the very marrow of his spirit were the last words he had had of Drehkos, ere they had left him locked in the Council Chamber with his comrades.

"It's possible that our cause *will* be defeated, brother mine. But if indeed it is, you'll have to follow your heathenish custom of succession and pass Horse Hall on to your eldest daughter's son. Even if I die, at least I'll have seen to it that your by-blow never profanes our father's place. That's right, dear loving brother, I ordered the execution of your precious Vaskos to be performed the moment we were out of sight of the hall!"

Each of them accompanied by a brace of Raikuh's men, Spiros and Hail had cut off crosscountry to alert Kindred families in the villages and smaller halls and to get them armed and headed toward Morguhn Hall. The rest rode the road in a tight military formation, preceded by vanguards and trailed by a strong rearguard, the flanks scouted by ranging outriders. But the return trip proved uneventful. Though they rode an important thoroughfare, bathed in the sunlight of a perfect spring day, they spied not another human, either on the road or in the fields. And that in itself was significant . . . and ominous.

As Bili and the vanguard cleared the entry tunnel and

rode into the outer courtyard, every sword within sight was raised in formal salute, such a salute as was rendered only to a highranking nobleman. He did not need to be told that his father had died during his absence and that, barring only the formality of Council approval, he was *Thoheeks* and Chief, in fact.

Old Sami hastened to hold his new master's stirrup, then bowed low, saying, "He went to Wind at the highest blaze of Sacred Sun, My Lord. The bards say that that is a most blessed time, if a chief cannot go to Wind in battle. We have clothed his husk appropriately and laid him in the great chamber, where your Lady Mothers bide with him. Shall I now conduct you there, Chief Bili?"

Bili shook his head curtly. "Later, Kinsman, I've much to do. For now, I want a fresh horse, one that can mindspeak better than this one. *Komees* Hari and Kinsman Feelos Pooleeos will be guesting with us. Also, as you can see, I've brought more Freefighters. There are two officers and twenty-seven men. Their commander is Captain Pawl Raikuh, a Harzburker and a gentleman. Lodge him in the Hall.

"Bard Klairuhnz has an important prisoner. Best let him be the judge of proper confinement. I'll want six of our own Freefighters who know the country roundabouts to ride with me on an immediate scout. See first to that and to having my gear transferred to the fresh horse. And have someone fetch me a big beaker of cool wine and a bucket of water. I'm all dust, inside and out."

Turning, he called over his brother. "Djehf, our father is gone to Wind; he lies in the great chamber. I think that I should scout the villages and the general vicinity before dark. You will be Chief until I return, but let *Komees* Djeen and Sami handle defense preparations. Sami knows this place from top to bottom and *Komees* Djeen has both besieged and been besieged, so he knows what to prepare for and against.

"See to the preparation of the pyre in the rear courtyard. It's just too crowded out here. For now, go in and render our respects to our mothers."

When answering Bili's summons, Djeen found himself saluting! Though less than a third his years, this boy was suddenly radiating authority, and it just seemed natural to accept that authority. "Your orders, My Lord?"

Bili acknowledged the salute, saying, "Lord *Komees,* shortly I will be taking a half-dozen troopers on a patrol of the surrounding area. My brother will be Chief in my absence. However, as I have just informed him, you and Kinsman Sami will share exclusive command of the troops, the Hall, and preparations for its defense, as well as arrangements for such Kindred as come here for refuge."

"It might be well that you closet with Bard Klairuhnz for as long a time as he needs to take the 'Lament of Clan Morguhn' from your memory. We will give Chief Hwahruhn's smoke to Wind at the return of Sun, tomorrow; and if Clanbard Hail is not back by that time, Bard Klairuhnz's services will be needed.

"Also, please have wagons and teams and guards for them ready. Choose the guards from among Captain Raikuh's men; they appear to be experienced looters. If there are no hostile forces in the hall village, I'll send back a messenger, and the wagons and men can come down and strip it of anything we can use."

At the time of the conquest of Northern Karaleenos by the Confederation, all land had belonged either to the king or the great nobles, who had resided only in the cities. Those who had lived on and worked the land had been accounted as much a part of it as the animals and crops; nor had their lives and well-being been considered of much importance by their owners, save as a source of revenue. Even then, over a hundred years agone, had they been a people of mixed antecedents—part Ehleen, part indigenous native.

With the settlements of the Horseclansmen, the old order had been drastically changed. The Kindred had been nomadic herdsmen for hundreds of years, and though in Karaleenos their felt-and-leather lodges were become stone halls, farming was to them an alien and despised occupation. They remained herdsmen, breeders of horses, cattle, goats, and sheep, taking what lands they needed for pasturage or for the sites of their halls. What was left was freely given to those who wished to farm as their own property, to use or dispose of as they should desire.

What few of the Ehleen nobility as were left slavishly copied this practice—indeed, copied any practice, no matter how barbaric in their own eyes, that would allow them to retain the remainder of their much reduced lands and stations. Things were more or less chaotic for a decade or two, until the former land slaves became adapted to the new order and their unaccustomed role of landowners, responsible only to themselves.

So had it been for over a hundred years. And as generations of the younger sons of Kindred Houses had wed the daughters of merchants, tradesmen, and farmers, while their titled brethren were blending their own blood and genes with scionesses of the houses of the surviving Ehleenoee nobility, there became less and ever less distinction between Kindred herder and Ehleenoe farmer stocks.

To *Komees* Djeen and most of the other so-called Kindred Nobles, it seemed incomprehensible—and smacked strongly of sorcery—that so large a proportion of the nonnoble classes should be involved in what had become an open revolt supposedly directed against the Kindred, for many of these very rebels had fully as much or even more Kindred blood than did the bulk of the nobles!

One did not, of course, have to sympathize with *Vahrohnos* Myros of Kehnooryos Deskati to understand at least some of the reasoning which underlay his treason. Before the defeat of Karaleenos and its forced merger with the Confederation, his ancestors had been overlords of three cities and three-quarters of the lands which now made up the Duchy of Morguhn, as well as parts of the neighboring Duchy of Vawn. This was not the first revolt spawned by the broodings of Ehleenoee minor nobility on past grandeurs, but it was the first in this part of Karaleenos in nearly a hundred years, as well as but the second in all of the Confederation to have such wide backing of the common sorts.

While the House of Deskatios had produced many highly intelligent men of rare talents and value to the Duchy and Confederation, it had also produced more than its share of scions who had been considered at least "odd" by their contemporaries. Indeed, Myros himself had once been a brilliant and promising officer in the Army of the Confederation until after over ten years of exemplary service, he had been suddenly relieved of his command, stripped of his military rank, and forbidden ever again to display his Fourth Class Silver Cat.

No one in all the Duchy ever admitted to knowing the truth in the matter, but there were rumors . . . one of them that had he not already succeeded to and been confirmed in his title, his neck would surely have made the short, sharp acquaintance of an Army executioner's sword, so grave had been his offense.

So Myros had scant reason to love the Confederation and at least some reason to envy the *Thoheeks* of Morguhn and Strahteegos *Komees* Djeen and even Substrahteegos-to-be Vaskos Daiviz, since all three held titles of which he felt himself to have been cheated. A return to the ancient order would therefore place him squarely in the very lap of his dreams.

But for the humbler sorts, a return to the ancient order—the bad old days—would be a return to the status of dumb, enslaved beast of burden. So none of the noble Kindred could fathom any gain these common folk might hope to secure in turning on their present rulers.

CHAPTER XI

The village of Hohryos Morguhn—service and garden village of Morguhn Hall—lay not quite two Ehleen kaiee from the Hall. Beyond it, a few hours by horse and half a day by wagon, lay the city of Kehnooryos Deskati, squarely athwart the north-south Traderoad and consequently the main commercial center of the Duchy.

The village was deserted, as Bili had felt it would be. But the evacuation had been very recent, for the blacksmith's forgefire still was very hot and a scytheblade, which had snapped while being straightened, was yet warm to the touch. All wagons and carts, all mules and oxen were missing, along with their owners, which meant that the villagers must have gone by road, and since the patrol had encountered not a single person on their ride down from the Hall, the people must have fled to Kehnooryos Deskati.

The young *Thoheeks* sent one of the troopers galloping back to the Hall to fetch the wagons and guards. It was a safe bet, considering the amount of loot they had appropriated along with the horses, that most of Pawl Raikuh's men were old hands at pillaging and could go through the outbuildings and the village's twenty-odd homes like the proverbial dose of salts.

By the roadside, just beyond the village, they found a savagely mutilated corpse. From its general build and masculature, they assumed it to be a man's body. There was no remaining way to tell the sex, much less the identity of the hacked, charred, incomplete carcass. Bili could only hope that the poor creature had been dead *before* the dreadful mutilations had been done.

Leaving the grisly discovery where it lay, Bili led his five troopers in a wide crosscountry sweep to the south and west. At the crest of the first hill, they spied a mounted party laboring up its south slope—half a dozen appeared to be women and twice that number well-armed men. As the party neared Bili's concealed position, he recognized the leader and trotted downslope to meet him.

"*Thoheek*'s-son Bili, you are a welcome sight to clap eyes to!" Vaskos reined up knee-to-knee and gripped Bili's hand with fierce geniality. The thick-thewed man had a few fresh cuts on his face, a bulky wad of bandage protruded from under his helm, and he rode somewhat stiffly, as if his armor might conceal other wounds, but he greeted Bili with a smile. "And how fares my father? Have you seen aught of him?"

The smile was infectious and Bili found himself sharing it. "*Komees* Hari is at Morguhn Hall, Vaskos, and he's well enough, physically; but sight of you will do wonders for his spirit. Your loving uncle, Drehkos, swore that he'd had you murdered, you know."

"Aye!" Vaskos's grin faded and his dark eyes clouded with anger. "His dogs and those of Hehrah-the-bitch very nearly did slay me, would have, but for the warning of my half sisters, bless them. My poor Frahnkos gave his life that the four of us might get away. We arrived at *Komees* Djeen's hall just after the Clanbard had left. Lady Ahnah and her women bandaged our hurts and provided me with armor, then they took over the care of my sisters and I took command of the mercen . . . uh, Freefighters."

After formally greeting the ladies of the party—Lady Ahnah, *Komees* Djeen's vivacious wife, her daughter, and the three Daiviz girls—Bili detached one of his troopers to guide Vaskos on the quickest route to the Hall, commandeering a brace of Vaskos's Freefighters to fill out the patrol.

When he had seen the refugees on their way, Bili instructed the troopers in the location of their rendezvous point, then all set out in a wide-spreading crescent. They rode on and on through the deserted fields, meadows, and woodlands. At the beginning, the westering sun bore upon their right, then directly into their faces, finally bathing their left sides. Bili allowed the new horse his head in walking across a freshly plowed field, then warily traversed a narrow strip of woods. He mounted grassy knolls at the trot, galloped over the rolling leas, leaping lichened fences and the deep-cut brooks which chuckled amongst rounded stones.

Then, all at once, the cold prickling began in Bili's fargathering mind and he knew that he was approaching a danger. Though it seemed imminent, it lacked the strength of human minds, so he did not uncase his axe, unslinging his boarspear instead.

He never had an opportunity to use that spear, however. Beneath the spread of a thick-foliaged old tree, a heavy form hurled itself down upon Bili, driving him from the saddle, smashing him to earth. The last sound he heard, ere darkness claimed him, was the terrified screaming of his horse.

It was with a sense of mild satisfaction that Hwahltuh Sanderz of Sanderz withdrew his hand from inside the waistband of his loose, filthy trousers. That pestersome flea would never again taste of blood. Absently, he wiped his thumbnail on a grimy shirtsleeve and ruminated on the journey so far.

True, the lands lay fair enough, but there were far too many people on them. It virtually teemed with people, and almost all of them were Dirtmen too, living—if such a life could be truly called living—in immovable lodges amid their own stink from birth to death. And the way that all of them stared and stared at him and his clansmen, especially at the Cat Brothers. Why, one might think that they had never before even seen Prairie Cats!

Even those who claimed the ancient Kinship with him—claimed descent from the Horseclansmen of Ehlai—dwelt in stonewalled lodges. Of course, he ruminated, he was not sure but that some of these had lied in their teeth, for only two of them had even looked like Kindred. One of these two, who had represented himself as the Kahrtuh of Kahrtuh, had had so little mindspeak that it would have been a great compliment to call his talents marginal—and what clan would have for Chief a man who could not mindspeak Cat and Horse and other Chiefs? As for the other, he had been *fat,* his hands as soft as a woman's breast.

But, Hwahltuh thought on, so much soaking in water the temperature of fresh blood might very well make a man that soft. And that was yet another thing that set the Sanderz's teeth edge-to-edge, the washings and scrubbings and senseless—and certainly unhealthful—bathings which seemed to so obsess these strange people. Although all the clanspeople made use of a sweatlodge on occasion, they seldom immersed their bodies in water more than a couple of times a year, and then it was in a river or lake. But the odd people of this weird land sometimes bathed twice in one *day,* and in heated water at that!

Hwahltuh had been born with a better than average nose—thank Sacred Sun for that gift! With eyes and ears hooded and stopped, he could identify each of his warriors by smell, alone. So it made him distinctly uneasy when he was confronted by persons who bore so little odor that he could rarely even distinguish the women from the men, without seeing or hearing them.

One of the clansmen riding behind him suddenly guffawed and it was picked up by several of the others; then came a snarled curse. He glanced back over his shoulder in time to see his sister's youngest son, Rik, leap from his kak, his hands working frantically at the drawstring of his trousers and his snubnosed face twisted in distress.

Hwahltuh halted the column, for it was not good to leave a Kinsman alone in unknown territory. Rik squatted beneath a tree, glaring at his Kinsmen from under his thick, reddish blond brows and grunting insulting comments on their appearances and personal habits, while they serenaded him with a chorus of jeers, laughter, and ribald suggestions.

The Sanderz shook his graying head in sympathy, for he too had suffered from that violent griping of the guts, as had they all, many times since they began to traverse this land. After discussion of the matter, they had decided that the problem was the dearth of decent food and the overabundance of wine. All their lives, they had been nurtured principally on the produce of their herds—milk and its products, flesh of cattle and sheep and goats. Although they sometimes traded (or raided) for dried beans or grain and the occasional pig, most of their accustomed plant foods had been wild, hunted as a matter of course, like game. The Chief could have counted upon the fingers of one hand the number of times he had tasted of wine, ere they had come to this land. Not that he and his did not like the stuff, but, Sun and Wind, it roiled the guts!

Rik had finished his business and was about to remount when Hwahltuh received the mindspeak of one of the three Cat Kindred who had been ranging ahead.

"Keep cased your bows, Brothers-of-Cats, for Whitetip comes with another Brother, a Chief!"

Bili was bereft of consciousness for but a moment, but his vision remained blurred longer, and he could not immediately tell just who or what had unhorsed him and was presently pinning him down with its considerable weight. He could hear points of some description rasping on his armor and there was a hot, acrid smell close to his face.

Abruptly, his vision cleared to disclose a cavernous red pink expanse of open mouth, equipped with a rough-looking tongue of incredible width and a full complement of big white teeth, crowned by a pair of glistening fangs at least three inches in length. Bili had never seen the like, but he knew from the very presence of those fangs that it could be no other animal but that one described in the ancient bardsongs.

Confidently, he mindspoke. "You would slay your Kinsman, Cat-brother?"

The heavy body started in surprise. "You mindspeak, then, Dirtman-who-wears-steel? This is truly a land of wonders."

"I must have erred," retorted Bili. "I had supposed you of the Cat Clan. A one of the true Clan of Cats would not seek the life of a Morguhn. So you most certainly are just an animal!"

The attacker rippled a snarl and the claws rasped again across Bili's breastplate. "Whitetip is no animal, Dirtman! He is a Cat of the Sept of Sanderz. But how is he to know that *you* are a Cat-brother?"

After a long moment of cudgeling his memory, Bili beamed, "I will care for your kittens and nursing females, and vouchsafe you a clean death when your teeth have dulled and the pains of age rest upon you."

The crushing weight lifted from Bili, while a four-inch width of sandpaper tongue gently scraped over his sweaty face. Stiffly, he sat up and stared at this creature of bardsong and legend.

The Cat's paws were large, as was the head, and intelligence sparkled in the amber depths of the eyes. The pelt was shortfurred, of a golden chestnut hue, with the ghosts of slightly darker rosettes speckling the graceful, muscle-rippling body. Whitetip stood a good nine hands at the withers and Bili estimated the weight at possibly three hundred pounds, for the Cat was bigboned, with a deep chest and forelegs much more thickly muscled than those of Treecats or lynxes. The white-tipped tail was short, its two feet or so giving him an overall length of some seven feet.

Seating himself nearby, Whitetip raised a paw to his fearsome mouth, licked it, and commenced leisurely washing his face, mindspeaking the while. "Ah, Kinsman, ever is it heartening to find a new Brother-of-Cats, especially so in such a new, strange land. But you are certainly the biggest Kinsman Whitetip has ever mindspoken . . . near nineteen hands, anyway. Are all of your Clan so large? How big is your Chief?"

"*I* am Chief," Bili informed the curious Cat. "I am Chief Bili, Morguhn of Morguhn."

Bili readily agreed to allow Whitetip to conduct him to his Chief, but pointed out that thanks to the big cat, he no longer had a horse. Contritely, the feline offered to find Chief Morguhn's mount and bring him back. Bili consented, though he doubted that such would come to pass, suspecting the gelding to be halfway to Kehnooryos Deskati by that time.

Therefore, he was rather surprised to see his horse trot placidly over the nearest hill less than ten minutes later, with Whitetip crouched awkwardly on the kak and two similar Cats loping along behind.

On introduction, the newcomers were disclosed to be: Lover-of-water, a female and three years older than Whitetip, though only some two-thirds of his size and weight; and Steelclaws, two years old and already nearly adult-size, a son out of the first litter sired by Whitetip.

After Bili had opened his mind to Clanbard Gil Sanderz, that middleaged warrior solemnly informed his Chief and clansmen, "All that has been mindspoken is true, Brothers. He is Morguhn of Morguhn of the Tribe of Ehlai and ruler of this land through which we now ride. But it is not so peaceful a land as we had thought. Chief Bili's stonelodge must soon be attacked by Dirtmen; he has need of every arm that can pull a bow!"

This last delighted the bored clansmen and the decision to ride with and fight for Chief Bili was unanimous. The whole of the ride to the tiny village of Geertohnee, at which the patrol had arranged to rendezvous, they laughed and joked and boasted and roared out warsongs, keeping time by clanging their saberblades against their targetbosses and twanging bowstrings over helms.

Not knowing who might choose to tap his thoughts, Bili sought to bury certain of them deeply—as deeply as possible—for he knew well that he needed the help these men offered; the addition of more than a dozen expert archers was indeed a gift of Sun. But he was appalled, shocked to the very core of his being, at the appearance of these latter-day Kindred Horseclansmen! He had known, of course, that his ancestors had been short men, but he had always supposed them to have been short as *Komees* Hari and the treacherous Duhkos were short—very broad and bigboned and thickthewed. Everything about the Sanderz men was small though—hands, feet, even heads—and he doubted if even the heaviest of them could possibly weigh more than sixty Ehleen kilohee. Furthermore, his new allies were undoubtedly the filthiest men he had ever seen—or *smelled*!

However, regardless of their heights or weights or degrees of cleanliness, they all handled and exuberantly tossed their well-kept weapons like men who had cut their teeth on such hardware. Their sabers were wide, single edged, thickbladed, and averaged some two-and-a-half feet around the slight curve. All bore the short, powerful, composite hornbows which were a hallmark of Horseclansmen; several had light axes dangling from the pommels of their beautifully worked and highly decorated kaks, and about half of them carried odd, almost uniform pole arms—a seven- or eight-foot shaft, mounting a knife-edged blade like the point of a boarspear at both ends. All the Sanderz's cuirasses were wrought of boiled leather, reinforced with strips of horn and metal, and lacquered. The helms of a few of the younger men were also of reinforced leather, but most wore steel helms of various shapes and patterns.

As for the "horses" of the clansmen, Bili thought that "ponies" would be a more accurate description of the ugly, shaggy, big-headed little steeds. The very tallest was no more than thirteen-two and some of them stood a full hand less! But their mindspeak talents were the best Bili had ever encountered and most seemed even more intelligent than Mahvros. And their size notwithstanding, they could clear any obstruction as easily as Bili's big bay hunter; nor did they indicate strain at maintaining the stiff pace.

The kaks were works of art. The wood and bone trees, covered with the finest leather, were set atop cured sheepskins and gorgeous blankets. Every visible inch of the leather was tooled and tinted and lacquered, the outside surfaces of the high, flaring cantles and pommels set with strips, studs and hooks of brass, silver, and polished steel. Bridles were nonexistent, since the mounts were guided solely by mindspeak and knee pressure.

The heel of Sacred Sun had sunk into the line of bluish haze which was the foothills of the Kahpneezon Mountains, when Bili had Hwahltuh and his clansmen halt within the concealment afforded by the woods which flanked the ploughlands of Geertohnee. At the older Chief's command, the three Cats set out to reconnoiter the village and its environs.

Presently, Whitetip was beaming back to both Chiefs, "Five men in this place. They wear steel, but it is not the same as Chief Bili's, being small pieces on leather shirts, like the scales of a fish. Whitetip thinks they have seen or smelled you, for they have hidden their horses and strung their bows and now face you across the open space. Shall we stampede their mounts and take the men in the rear, while you attack?"

"No!" Bili hastily mindspoke. "For they are almost certainly my fighters, Cat-brother, though there should be six, not five." Then to Hwahltuh, "They are watching for me alone, so let me ride in first. I will signal you." With that, he rode out into the open.

Only the tiniest, copperhued arc of Sacred Sun still showed above the western mountain haze when the *Thoheeks* and his band came within sight of Morguhn Hall. The stout little bastion lay already invested by the rebellious rabble, whose broad track the three cats and eighteen horsemen had cautiously paralleled for near two hours.

Forty yards from the main gate sat a wagon-mounted ram blazing merrily, while the slope roundabout the front and the west side of the hall was randomly littered with discarded shields, weapons, scaling ladders, and some twoscore arrowquilled bodies, very few of these within fifty yards of their objective. And Bili breathed a sigh of relief. At least the initial assault had been rebuffed . . . bloodily rebuffed.

Just beyond bowshot of the walls and towers, mounted nobles were slowly and painfully reforming their heterogeneous mob for a second attack. That it was a difficult job was attested by the shouted obscenities, screams of profane rage, and the *thwacks* of ridingwhips and swordflats which were clearly audible to the watchers.

The rebels were an army in name only. They had just seen friends and neighbors and relatives suffer or die on the now gory path to those forbidding walls, and their priests and officers had yet to convince them that another sally against those bristling fortifications would result in aught save ever more wounds and deaths. Those who had for so long secretly drilled them and taught them weapons usage, they now felt, had unjustly kept from them the hard facts of warfare—the utter exhaustion and dry-mouthed terror which so weighted a man's limbs when he saw of what horrors arrows and darts and catapult stones were capable.

Thick black smoke roiled up from within the walls and the lowing of cattle could be plainly heard, along with the creaking of ropes and groaning of timbers as a catapult was wound and set. After a brief pause, there was a *wheee-WHUNNK* and a headsized blob of burning pitch traced a high, smoketrailing parabola across the darkening sky, to fall squarely into the milling midst of the rebel 'formation'! It was all that the priests and nobles could then do to prevent an outright rout. Wisely, they elected to form several hundred yards farther away.

Bili, Hwahltuh, Gil, and one of the Freefighters slid down from their observation point at the brushy summit of a hill. The Sanderz snorted his disgust at the quality of the men opposing them.

"Kinsman Bili, a stand of prairiegrass would slow us more than cowards like those. Let us ride through them now."

But Bili shook his shaven head. "No, we are too many to just ride up to the walls, especially since it is now almost dark. My clansmen and Freefighters are expecting no more than seven riders. When they spied a party of this size, they surely would bring us under their bows. We must find a way to let them know that we are friends. Are any of your clansmen far-speakers, by chance?"

"Ask anything but that, Kinsman," groaned Hwahltuh. "I heard that that talent is common amongst the folk of some clans, but our last far-speaker went to Wind when I was yet a lad. Whitetip can farspeak, to a limited extent, but only, alas, if he knows the mind to which he is to beam."

Gil spoke up. "If there are mindspeakers in the stonelodge, why not wait until full dark and let a Cat-brother go close enough to range them?"

Atop the front wall, amidst the archers and catapult crews, old *Komees* Djeen limped stiffly up and down, snapping and snarling at all and sundry out of his worry over the fate of *Thoheeks* Bili. The wagons were long since returned before even the van of the rebel host had appeared. Since Vaskos was the last man to have clapped eyes on Bili, he had suffered questioning and requestioning by the retired Strahteegos, until at length the Keeleeohstos—grumpy anyway at being bedridden by order of Master Ahlee—had bluntly inquired as to which his questioner was actually losing, his hearing or his memory. And the Lady Ahnah and *Komees* Hari had had to be fetched, ere the shouting and insults were done, to persuade the two officers to keep their steel cased!

His threequarter armor clanking, the grizzled nobleman stalked up to a group of fledgling engineers being put through a crash course in catapult service. "You!" he barked at a tall Freefighter who was lowering a fifty-pound stone into the basket. "Don't you know better than to wear a crested helm when you're serving an engine? If the lip of that basket hooks that crest, it'll take the empty head off your shoulders. I've seen it happen, soldier!"

Not awaiting an answer, he swung off to confront an archer seated in a crenel. "*Behind* a merlon, fool! Keep sitting between them and you'll have an arrow up your arse or in your back! And replace that bowstring immediately. It's beginning to fray at the lower curve."

"If Bili's not back soon," muttered Spiros to Bard Klairuhnz, "we'll have to give Djeen a horse and let him go searching for that patrol, ere he rides these men into mutiny! Next, he'll be ordering them to polish all the fornicating spearpoints, or having them down there aligning all the cattle by height, sex, and age!"

"There'll be no mutiny here, My Lord," stated Captain Raikuh, who was standing with them near the gate tower. "As is Duke Bili, so is Count Djeen. Both are born warleaders, and all the professionals can sense the fact. His words may ring harsh, but his criticisms are both sound and constructive, and we all know it."

A thousand yards from the west wall on the creekbank, wagons and wains were unloading tents and gear amid a twinkling of torches and new-kindled fires. At long last, the priests and nobles had despaired of whipping their cowed aggregation of commoners into mounting another assault . . . not this night, at least. Even to those at the hall it was clear that the rebels had had enough for one day and were going into camp.

Spiros was still worried and annoyed by Djeen's ceaseless nitpicking at the men, so he sought to distract the old soldier, calling, "*Komees* Djeen, if you please? Djeen, come over here and tell us, do you think they'll come for us again tonight?"

Yellow teeth glinting, the old man cackled harshly. "I only wish that they would, Kinsman! You would then see what disastrous effects flaming pitchballs and firearrows have on the morale of undisciplined troops at night. Heh, heh. That piss-poor excuse for an army wouldn't stop running until they reached the Sea of Grass, most likely. But no, Spiros, they'll not attack tonight, for men who lack the grit to fight in broad day will murder their officers before they'll mount a night offensive."

His lobstertail neckguard grated on his backplate as he slowly shook his head. "That damned boylover Myros . . . d'you know, he was a middling-good officer, once upon a time? But did you see the inexcusable way he marshaled that abortion of an assault? Clear it is, he's long since forgot every principle of tactics he ever learned!"

Winking slyly at Raikuh and Klairuhnz, Spiros innocently asked, "Your pardon, Djeen, but I thought they came up that hill in pretty fair form . . . of course, I'm no professional soldier . . ."

"True enough, Kinsman!" snapped the *Komees*. "Were you, you'd have been painfully aware of the glaring errors of judgment of which the *Vahrohnos* of Pederasty was guilty. He'd no need to lose either his engine or half the men we slew, you know? Here, let me show you what I mean . . ."

Drawing a short dagger from the top of his boot, he stumped over to a section of tower wall between two torches, and commenced to scratch a rough sketch on the surface of the stones, talking all the while. Spiros, his purpose now achieved, was careful to ape meticulous attention to each detail of the aged Strahteegos's discourse. Raikuh on the other hand hung on every word, feeling personal instruction from so famous and respected a strategist and tactician to be a rare privilege.

Klairuhnz wandered away from the absorbed nobleman and his little audience to stand beside young Djehf, who leaned between a pair of merlons, staring at the bright, bustling camp of the besiegers.

"Didn't you hear *Komees* Djeen's admonition to that archer, Kinsman?"

Half turning, the Tahneest clanked the side of his gauntlet against his breastplate. "This be good, honest Pitzburk plate, and princegrade, at that! Good Bard, the bowman's unspawned who can put a shaft through such metal."

Klairuhnz smiled thinly. "Be not too sure, Kinsman. I've seen Horseclansmen stipple an armored man until he looked like a porcupine! Why, on the Prairie, once . . ."

A note of eagerness entered the young warrior's voice, and out of that eagerness peeped the small boy of recent memory. "You've really ridden with *real* Horseclansmen then, Kinsman? On the Prairie? The Sea of Grass? Truly? Tell me, please, tell me of them."

"Yes," stated the Bard. "Yes, I rode the Prairie with Horseclansmen, Kinsman Djehf, but it was long, long years ago, and I . . ."

His voice stopped as the unexpected and quite powerful mindspeak burst in. "I know *your* mind, Cat-brother-of-

Cat-brothers, who these men know as Bard Klairuhnz. This one is Whitetip, Subchief of the Cat Sept of Sanderz. We mindspoke in the south, in the hot land."

In the rear courtyard of Morguhn Hall, Bili lifted his cased axe from his weary mount, before an armed servant led the gelding away. Silent but for the clank of his armor, he paced over to Mother Behrnees and kissed her freckled forehead, then took her hand, saying, "Come, Mother, I wish you to meet our new friends."

He led her over to the knot of curiously staring clansmen and halted before Gil and the Chief. "Chief Hwahltuh of Sanderz, allow me to present one of my Lady Mothers. This is My Lady Behrnees of Morguhn, widow of my late father, Hwahruhn Morguhn of Morguhn, and presently cochatelaine of Morguhn Hall."

Hwahltuh immediately knew that this tall, blond beauty was the loveliest woman he had ever before seen. Everything about her was perfect, he thought, and no dream that he could recall had produced even a vision like to that now before him. He knew that he should speak, acknowledge the introduction, introduce Gil and the others, but with his mind awhirl with thoughts totally removed from the torchlit courtyard, he was experiencing difficulty in framing words.

Before he could regain his control, Behrnees stepped forward, took his callused, grubby hand, and bore it to her seemingly perfect pink lips, saying gravely, "My sincere thanks, Lord Hwahltuh, for bringing my son safely back to us. We all are in your debt. Come, you and your Kinsmen must sup with us ere you leave. But leave you must, for this hall lies invested by a great host, with no hope of reinforcement or aid."

When the clan had decided to leave the high plains and rejoin their Kindred who had trekked east, Hwahltuh had had three wives. But over the course of the long, difficult, dangerous journey, all these had gone to Wind, one by one. For three years now had he relied on the widows of his sons to see to the Chief's lodge, taking such pleasures as he desired of borrowed concubines, for the Couplets of the Law forbade marriage within the clan and custom forbade an unmarried man to hold ownership of concubines. And he was a lonely man. Until that moment, he had not realized just how lonely.

"I'll be more than happy to share milk and meat with you, Kinswoman, and so too will my Kindred. But why this talk of leaving, before we've even bloodied our sabers? My Clan-brothers and I, we were promised a good fight by your son, Chief Bili, and . . . What is this, Kinswoman? Are you ill?"

Behrnees had dropped to her knees before him, once more pressing her shellpink lips to his scarred, filthy knuckles.

Bili enlightened the mystified, and more than a little perturbed Chief. "In my Lady Mother's homeland, homage is so rendered, Hwahltuh."

Behrnees, taller and with bigger bones, probably weighed as much as did the Sanderz, but the little man grasped her shoulders and lifted her slowly and without apparent strain, saying gruffly, "It is *I* who am guesting in *your* lodge, Kinswoman. Nor am I your Chief. You owe me no homage."

Behrnees met his eyes with her limpid blue ones and he felt his heart beating very fast under his cuirass, felt his weatherbrowned face flushing, found his breath as short as if he had been fighting all day . . . and found his hands very loath to release those well-muscled but so pleasant-to-hold shoulders.

Humbly Behrnees said, "I would do homage to your courage, My Lord. Your wives and your sons know much pride in so strong and valiant a husband and father."

Now Gil had been slyly prying into the unshielded minds of both his chief and the woman. He recognized the utter sincerity of her admiration of Hwahltuh, as well as the Sanderz's quite different admiration of her. She certainly was not an old woman—he estimated her age at no more than thirty-four summers—was a more than handsome female, threw good get if Chief Bili was any indication, and was the widow of a Chief. He thought that the Clan might go far and far without finding any better wife for their Chief. So he stepped forward.

"Chief's mother, I am Gil, Clanbard of Sanderz, and I am indeed proud of my Chief, as are all his Clan-Brothers. But as you are a widow, so is he a widower. He has had no wife for near three summers, and all his strong sons went to Wind in honor and to the glory of their Clan."

Behrnees's eyes misted. She drew closer to Hwahltuh, and when he tilted back his head to keep sight of her face, she laid a hand alongside one of his stubbled, dust-grimy cheeks and softly lipbrushed the other, saying gently, "I grieve with and for you, Kinsman. When time and the enemy allow, we must try to comfort each other."

And from that moment, Hwahltuh Sanderz of Sanderz was hers, heart and soul! With her by his side, he moved as in a blissful dream, greeting Chief Bili's brother and his father's other widow and the remaining notables. Her delicate, subtly feminine odor was, he knew, the sweetest scent to which his keen nose had ever attained.

Even when he was conducted to another of those cursed washingplaces and the herbed and spiced bathwater—steaming like a bucket of fresh milk on a winter morning—enveloped him and the servants began to scrub him, did he keep his peace, his mind too filled with Behrnees to even think the curses and threats which he had heretofore blasted at bathservants. For the first time in his nearly fifty years of life, Hwahltuh was in love.

Only one good had come out of the day, so far as Myros was concerned. Thoroughly trounced and resultantly cowed as they were, his ill-disciplined mob at least obeyed orders and followed instructions with unaccustomed alacrity. Therefore, as soon as the tents were up and the rabble fed on jerked meat, hard bread, strong cheese, and weak, vinegary wine, he had them set to assembling the six big catapults, making pitchballs and scaling ladders and collecting stones from up and down the streambed. He had hoped to capture Morguhn Hall without too much structural damage to the place—with that loudmouthed fool, Paulos, choked to death on his own blood and teeth back in the Council Chamber, there would now be no questions concerning the new ownership of the hall. He felt a slight gratitude to the hulking Djehf Morguhn—but now realized that he would probably have to burn or batter down a fair stretch of those walls, ere he could use his large but unwieldy and very undependable force to any advantage.

While whip-snapping overseers kept the commoners at their assigned tasks, Myros retired to his spacious pavilion, there to dine and confer with his fellow concilmen, his military subordinates, and the higher-ranking clergy. Of the Council, there were but three remaining to sit with him—Drehkos, Djaimos, and Nathos Evrehos, now recovered from his morning funk and hysterics and prating loudly of bloody deeds to be wreaked upon the persons of any Kindred taken alive.

As each of his guests came under his roof of golden silk, Myros's servants helped them out of their hot armor and sweatsoaked clothing, sponged their sweaty bodies, and proffered soft tunics and big mugs of chilled wine, a soothing balm to shouted-raw throats and a strong soporific for jangled nerves. By the time the viands—juicy roasts, savory vegetables, crisp salads, breads, and delicate pastries—were served, most of the guests were at least a bit tiddly.

Half through the meal, Myros was called to his headquarters-tent that he might receive a messenger. He returned wreathed in smiles, to announce:

"Gentlemen, three days ago did the True Faith triumph in what the heathens call the Duchy of Vawn!" He allowed the drunken cheering and hubbub to continue for a few minutes, then raised a hand for silence. "Wait, Brothers-in-God, there is more. The Army of the Faithful saw a miracle in Vawn. As our brethren held the cities and countryside, the sinful pagans fled to a very strong hall built into the side of a steep cliff. Only one side could be attacked, and it was protected by a wall so high and thick than an entire week of hurling stones against it did no real damage. Then did the men of weak faith talk most shamefully of forsaking the Holy Cause.

"But the Most Holy *Kooreeos* Marios did pray mightily that our loving Father might deliver into his hands the cursed heathens. And the Lord answered the Blessed Marios, sending an Angel to instruct him. Then were certain Sacred objects placed in a casket of iron, laid in the basket of the largest engine and hurled against that unholy wall. The very moment that the hallowed missile touched the wall of the place of sinfulness, did all the land tremble to God's awful Voice. Though the Lord allowed no man to see the bolt, His lightning did shatter the wall of the unbelievers, did rend stone from huge stone and crumble them to dust. And all of those heathen within were slain in a moment, most with no wound upon their bodies, yet with blood having gushed from every orifice.

"And that victorious army, led by the Most Blessed *Kooreeos* Marios, is marching to our aid. Even now is the bulk of their force crossing our western border, while the Holy Marios and their cavalry will be amongst us within the hour!"

Within Morguhn Hall, however, the evening meal was a most subdued one. At the lengthened high table were most of the loyal Kindred still alive in the Duchy. Bili, in the center chair, was flanked by his mothers. Djehf was on the walls, along with old *Komees* Djeen, Feelahks Sami, and Lieutenant Krahndahl. Beyond Mother Behrnees, who sat at the young *Thoheeks*'s right, Chief Hwahltuh happily applied himself to a shoulder of mutton and a brimming flagon of fresh, creamy milk. At his right, Eeyohahnah Daiviz sipped watered wine, toyed with her food, and pouted, since the handsome young Rik Sanderz seemed more interested in his disgusting dish of chopped meat and curds than he did in her. Actually, Hwahltuh's nephew was mindspeaking with Spiros and Pawl Raikuh, regaling them with gory anecdotes of the trek from the high plains.

On Rik's right were the other Daivizes—*Komees* Hari, the two younger girls, and the heavily bandaged Vaskos, on whom all three were lavishing so much attention that the Keeleeohs was embarrassed.

At Mother Mahrnee's left was *Vahrohnos* Spiros, and beside him the Lady Ahnah Morguhn. Between her and her daughter, Sairuh, sat Clanbard Gil Sanderz, patiently answering questions of mother and child, both evincing interest in every facet of the lives of the females of his clan. On the left of the girl, Captain Raikuh wolfed roast mutton and pickled cabbage, gulped wine, and occasionally chuckled at young Rik's stories.

Dark, dour Komos Morguhn, Bili's second cousin and though Kindred not really a nobleman, hulked between Bard Klairuhnz and Master Ahlee. That day, Komos had seen a pack of his neighbors, some of them related to him, senselessly butcher his wife, his children, and his aged, crippled father. Only the fortuitous arrival of Clanbard Hail and his two troopers in the village had saved the farmer; and the fact that he had been able to get to his grandfather's sword and fight off his attackers until his rescue. He had spoken to no one throughout the meal, nor had aught save wine passed his lips. He sat staring at his winecup, clenching and unclenching his big, work-roughened hands.

Trestle tables had been arranged around the walls of the large chamber and thereon dined the off-duty troops, serving themselves as did the very nobles, since all the servants were either in armor among them or chained in the cellars. So because the surroundings were so noisy, Bili attempted to mindspeak his scarcely known cousin.

But Bard Klairuhnz beamed. "Apparently, Kinsman Komos is not a mindspeaker, Thoheeks Bili. However, I took the liberty of scanning his mind earlier, and he knows not one whit more than he has recounted. He and the trooper who escorted him rode directly here; Hail and the other trooper rode for the hall of Lord Bahr Morguhn.

"My Lord, Clanbard Hail is presently either dead, captured, or safe. In any case, there's nothing that you or any of us can do for him, and Wind knows, you've more than sufficient worry material, without taking on that as well!"

"But it was my order sent him out, Kinsman," Bili silently replied. "Perhaps I should have sent a younger man . . . or gone myself."

"Nonsense, Lord *Thoheeks!* It was *your* duty to command and *his* duty to obey." Bard Klairuhnz seemed about to add more when he was interrupted.

Lieutenant Krahndahl had hurried into the room, helm under his arm and unease wrinkling his seamed face. The scales of his plain hauberk clashed as he rapidly rounded the high table and first bowed to Bili, then bent and whispered a brief message into the young lord's ear. His message spoken, he stepped back and assumed the posture of attention.

Bili did not need to call for silence, for all noise had ceased upon the appearance of the officer. He stood and announced, "My people, *Komees* Djeen reports a spate of activity within the lines of the enemy. Such could presage an attack, so we had best to the walls."

An immediate clatter and bustle ensued at the high and lower tables, a metallic din that commenced as armor doffed for the meal was redonned and adjusted, swordcases were snapped to belt or baldric, and helms were dragged from beneath the tables.

All at the high table had arisen. Bili caught Lieutenant Krahndahl's eye and gestured at the armor rack which held his scarred Pitzburk. "Please help me to arm, Krahndahl." Then he turned back to the table and its group.

"Chief Hwahltuh, you and your clansmen will report to my Subchief, *Komees* Djeen. He commands the walls and will place you all where your bows will do the most good." The wiry little man nodded once, slapped on his helm, and stepped briskly toward the door, mindcalling his kinsmen.

Bili strode down the length of the table to where Ahlee and Klairuhnz, having despaired of locating a cuirass big enough, were buckling an outsize brigandine, a pair of greaves, and a set of oldfashioned armlets over the powerfully convex chest and the rolling-muscled limbs of Cousin Komos.

"Kinsman Klairuhnz, you know that I well know your value as a warrior, so I beg you not take offense at the post I would have you fill. I had intended said post for Kinsman Vaskos, he being wounded, ere I was informed of his training and skills in use of engines, of which our garrison owns little enough. I charge you with the magazines, the dungeons, and their occupants. Two of our older servingmen will assist you. Should our foes enter the hall itself, you must strongly secure the cellar entry, slay every prisoner, and set fire the stores. Do you understand?"

At the Bard's curt nod, he turned to Komos. "Cousin, you are not trained to arms, but Sun has granted you great strength. Therefore, report you to Kinsman Vaskos and say that you are to help serve the engines. I doubt that a sixty-pound boulder will be any unchancy burden for your thews.

"Master Ahlee, summon your people and take your place on the walls."

He continued to issue crisp orders. Ahnah Morguhn was set to supervising those women and girls who were stoking the fires under great cauldrons of oil, water, and iron trays of sand in the outer courtyard. Mother Mahrnee took charge of a half-dozen more women, putting them to fletching and heading arrows, while Mother Behrnees formed a similar group to melt lead and cast sling bullets.

Within ten minutes of the lieutenant's entry, the dining hall lay deserted.

Klairuhnz unlocked the heavy door, stepped into the tiny cell, and thrust the butt of his torch into the wall bracket. *Kooreeos* Skiros awkwardly struggled to a sitting posture, his movements painfully hampered by the weight and placement of his iron fetters and chains. His black silken robes were dust stained and his hair and beard were matted; but his black eyes still shot out their message of defiance and bottomless hatred.

Leaning his saber against the wall, well out of the prisoner's reach, the Bard put his back to the door and sank onto his haunches, then thrust a hand under his brigandine and withdrew the weapon he had taken from Skiros. Depression of a stud on one arm of the "club" caused a steel box to slide smoothly out of that arm and plop into his hand. At one end of the box was a fat brass cylinder, flat on one end and dully pointed on the other. He regarded box, cylinder, and "club" for several moments, then slid the box back into place.

Speaking in the language of the Confederation, he asked, "What is your name? Your real name, that is."

"All men here know me, heathen." The *Kooreeos'* deep, rich baritone boomed hollowly in the narrow, high-ceilinged cubicle. "I am Skiros, *Kooreeos* of . . ."

"Cut the crap, chum!" Klairuhnz had not spoken the

language he now used in many years, except in his dreams, so his speech was slightly halting. Nevertheless, its effect on Skiros was instantaneous. Paling visibly, the cleric recoiled, as if from a buffet.

But he recovered quite rapidly, replying in Old Ehleeneekos, "I cannot understand you, heathen dog. Try barking in a civilized tongue!"

The Bard vented a humorless laugh. "Oh, you understand me, right enough, witchman. Just as the late Titus Backstrom understood, as the late Lillian Landor would have understood, as Doctor Manuel Kornblau understands!" He grasped the small "club" by the arm which contained the small box and squinted down the other arm at the prisoner, his thumb pulling back a grooved protrusion of metal with a sharp click.

"How many of these little toys have you scattered about this Duchy, witchman? Or are they reserved as a last resort for your kind only?"

"I'd appreciate it if you'd not point that gun at me. It's a twelve-point-five millimeter magnum, you know, one of the Center's developments, and powerful enough to punch through plate armor or stop a charging bison bull. The shock alone would stop the heart of this body, no matter where it was struck." Skiros's manner was relaxed, conversational. His language however, would have been meaningless to anyone in the duchy save his listener, since he spoke a cultured, nondialectal twentieth-century American English!

Klairuhnz smiled broadly. "So, Reverend Bishop, you really are a witchman, eh? Now, once again, what's your name?"

"Gold," the blackbeard answered easily. "William Gold. And you? You must be one of the mutants. Which one, may I ask?"

The Bard nodded. "Yes, Mr. Gold, you may ask. I'm Milo Moray."

Gold's eyes widened. "Well I'll be damned! The Undying God of the Horseclans himself. Then I'll not ask why you're here. I'll just assume that Manny was one of the 'lucky ones' who made it to Kehnooryos Atheenahs alive. But, tell me, is he still alive or have you killed him, too?"

Milo's head bobbed again. "When last I saw him, he lived. Of course, he wasn't any too comfortable. In addition to the alterations which were performed on him in Gafnee, because of his mindshield and his stubbornness—which latter quality I am glad to see you don't share—my persuasion specialists were required to perform some rather extreme exercises upon his body."

"Damn!" spat Gold. "You're as much a barbarian as the swine you root among!"

"Barbarism is a survival trait in this world," Milo smiled. "It has been for several hundred years . . . or didn't you ivory-tower boys know? Yes, Father Gold, I am a barbarian, but before you throw any more such epithets my way, be damned sure your own conscience is clean. This Old Time Religion you clowns have dreamed up is far more bloodthirsty and barbaric than anything these people have developed on their own!"

A hint of his sanctimonious facade crept back into the prisoner's tone. "We are simply striving to reestablish the faith which you so ruthlessly suppressed in the course of the last century, Moray."

"In a pig's ass!" snapped Milo. "For all that its fat-cat hierarchy were secretly engaged in such little sidelines as slavetrading, whoremongering, and smuggling—not to mention oppressing the humbler Ehleenoee with a quasi-military, quasi-religious masked force of bravos who would have made the sixteenth-century Spanish Garduna look like a troop of Boy Scouts—their religion was basically Eastern-rite Christianity. Yours sounds more like Satanism, what with the carving up of helpless children on your altars, the mixing of their lifeblood with the wine for your so-called Communion, and all the other obscene parodies of worship you engage in."

The chained man shrugged, his face expressionless. "If a pack of hounds serve you well, you endeavor to keep them contented. Most of our worshipers are well pleased with this kind of religion."

"I suspect," said Milo wryly, "that those fools are less enchanted by your sanguinary religion than they are by the utopian promises with which you've been deluding them. Need I ask what the hell you and your fellow ghouls are up to?"

In lieu of answers, the prisoner abruptly asked, "How old are you, Moray? When were you born, was it before the War?"

Milo did not need to ask which war, because for the few who had survived it, there could be but the one—that three-day holocaust which had irrevocably wrecked the civilization of their world and the worldwide plagues which had almost extirpated all the races of mankind. He shrugged. "I think I was born sometime around the turn of the century . . . the twentieth century, that is. That would put my age at a bit less than nine hundred years. Why?"

The manacles clanked as Gold steepled his fingers. "That means, Moray, that you were alive at the very apogee of man's culture and scientific achievements. Wouldn't you like to see the reestablishment of that culture and most of its appurtenances and civilized comforts?"

He leaned as far forward as his chains would permit, his black eyes gleaming, his voice now husky with his fervor. "Can't you understand, Moray? We at the J. and R. Kennedy Memorial Center are all that's left of The United States of America. We are simply trying to perform the patriotic duty of any good citizens: to bring about the recovery of our country. *Our* country, Moray, yours and mine! As it was before the War. Cities—real cities, man—research facilities, laboratories, universities, hospitals, electricity, flush toilets, automobiles, theatres, television, telephones, newspapers. Think of it, Moray!"

Milo cracked a knuckle aimlessly. "No sale, Gold. I've heard that spiel before from your director, when I spoke with him on the Landor woman's radio a hundred years ago. He told me all about your plans to establish a dictatorship and call it by the name of a long-dead republic. I want no part of such infamy! I warned him at that time to keep his parasites out of my lands. For your sake and for the sakes of those others he sent to trespass and agitate, I'm sorry he chose not to listen to me."

"I cannot, just cannot understand you, Moray," sighed Gold. "Why on earth are you so antagonistic toward us? We should be allies, should be working together, since we're so much alike, have so much in common."

Milo's expression became ugly. "*I* have nothing in common with *you,* Gold!"

The prisoner smiled warmly. "Of course you have, my good Moray. After all we are both of us immortal. In that way, at least, you are like me and I am like you."

A strong shudder coursed the length of Milo's body and utter loathing weighted his voice, reflected on his face as well. "No, Gold, not like me, never like me! *I* did nothing to bring about my longevity, nor did those who truly are like me. Our differences from ordinary humans are the gifts of Nature. The long lives of you and your ilk could not be less natural! You really deserve the appellation 'witchmen,' you know. Although I think that 'vampires' might be a better term.

"Yes, you've lived as long as I have, maybe longer, but in those seven or eight hundred years, how many vibrant young bodies have you personally usurped, Gold? In even one hundred years' time, how much human flesh and blood is needed to keep a warped, demonic thing like you alive?"

"Two, sometimes three transfers are necessary for survival of the mind, barring illness or accident. In the early days, it was a more frequent process, of course; but since we commenced selective breeding for strength, health and longevity . . . and also, we strive to take exceedingly good care of our bodies, Moray.

"You see, the process of mind displacement and transference is not a pleasant experience. Generally, it requires hours to days of suffering to accomplish, so naturally we don't look forward to repeating it any more often than is absolutely necessary."

"You're lying, Gold," snapped Milo. "I *saw* Titus Backstrom effect a transfer within minutes! And God knows how many times Lillian Landor switched back and forth from King Zastros's body to her own. If you're going to start trying to get cute, buster, I might be smart to drug your next meal . . . and keep you semiconscious until I get you back to Kehnooryos Atheenahs."

The fetters jangled as the prisoner raised his hands conciliatorily. "Wait just wait a minute, Moray, you don't fully comprehend."

Milo, on the point of arising, settled back against the door. "Okay, so tell me, Reverend Father."

Gold held out his arms, painfully working back the wide iron cuffs to expose the raw, bleeding flesh beneath. "First of all, Moray, why don't you take these things off me. Can't you see what they're doing to this body? Tetanus can kill just as surely as a sword, and I could tell you damned little if I contract lockjaw. I'll not try to escape, you have my word on it. Besides, you have my pistol."

Milo's shoulders rose and fell in a shrug. "As it happens, I can't. The castellan has the keys and he's on the walls. But even if I could, I wouldn't. You see, I've had sufficient experience with your kind to recognize just how slippery you are. As for your word, I'd not trust you any farther than I could throw my warhorse!"

The prisoner grinned ruefully. "Well, I did try. But it doesn't really matter. I'll be free soon enough. Do you think your fellow mutants would trade Manny—assuming that he *is* still alive—for you?"

"Anything is possible, Gold," Milo chuckled. "But

aren't you counting your chickens before they're hatched? I've seen weaker fortifications than these, manned by less well armed and less experienced fighters, stand off forces far superior to that ragtag horde of cannonfodder you and the *Vahrohnos* Myros have scraped up for your little *Djeehahd*. I'll be charitable and say only that they are not firstclass troops . . . or second-, or even third-. Their only assault so far was smashed a full fifty yards from the walls, and nothing the officers and priests could do or say persuaded them to mount another, so they've gone into camp.

"Saddled with amateur officers and without you to harangue them into a religious frenzy, your troops are impotent against this stout little garrison. No, your peasant crusaders will be good for no more than one more fullscale assault. Then the bulk of the survivors will desert and the diehards will hole up in Morguhnpolis or, possibly, Deskati. Whichever city they choose, the Confederation siege train will have its gates down and its walls breached in short order."

Gold threw back his head and chortled merrily. "Not quite, my good Moray, not quite! Now it is you who are counting chickens. The walls of this pitiful dungheap will be flat to the ground and its gates blown to smithereens before noon tomorrow, and there's not a damned thing you can do to prevent it either! And don't hold your breath until your precious Confederation Army gets here, for we've not been letting a living soul *out* of this Duchy for weeks, so you couldn't have gotten any message to them . . . not without a radio, anyway."

Milo replaced the pistol under his brigandine, stood erect, and locked his saber into the frog of his baldric. "You obviously know far less than you think you do about me and my people, Gold. When I get you back to Kehnooryos Atheenahs, we'll resume our little chat, unless a streak of stubbornness arises, in which case I'll see that you make the acquaintance of the artisans who cured the mulishness of your friend Manny."

He jerked the torch from the bracket and left the dank cell, slamming the heavy door and securing the thick bar in place, leaving Gold alone in the unrelieved darkness.

Under the travel-stained canvas of an officer-model campaign tent, on a narrow folding cot, lay a woman. She was strikingly lovely, with the red-gold flame of the watchlantern casting highlights throughout the glossy mane of blue black hair which framed her fine-boned face. Her lips were full and dark red, and although her long, sooty lashes lay upon her light olive cheeks and the proud swell of her firm breasts rose and fell rhythmically, she was not sleeping.

On the farspeak level of her infinitely complex and highly trained mind, she asked, "Where have you been? I knew not but that you'd drowned or smothered. If the men and cats and horses hadn't been so done in, we'd have marched on tonight. I thought you said you'd contact me at least once each day."

"Sorry, Aldora, but it couldn't be helped," beamed Milo's thought. "You know my farspeak won't range more than ten or twelve miles, even under optimum conditions. So without the use of Major Ahndros's fine mind . . ."

The woman's thought then became halting and tinged with pain. "Ahndee? He . . . he's dead, then? So . . . so young and vital and . . . and sweet."

"No, Aldora, not dead, not yet, but according to Master Ahlee, it's still touch-and-go. There was a nasty little skirmish the evening I last spoke with you. He wasn't really hurt too badly, but he went into shock before Ahlee got to him and the good doctor is now afraid to let him stay conscious for very long at one time."

"Whom are we speaking through then?" she inquired.

"The handsome, young heir to old Hwahruhn you mentioned? He truly does have farspeak, then?"

"Bili is now *Thoheeks,* my dear. Hwahruhn is gone to Wind. And I feel sure he has much, much more than just farspeak. Even without training, he may well be a very valuable man, though I've had no chance to make certain. You see," he went on, "a great deal has happened here in a very short time; things are moving much faster than we'd anticipated, much faster than they'd been planned to go, unless that bastard, Kornblau, misled us . . . and there's always that possibility. Actually, I'm contacting you through the mind of one of the Sanderz Sept Prairie Cats, Whitetip."

"Thank Sun and Wind!" Aldora mindspoke vociferously. "There's been too much inbreeding in recent years and more and more kittens are being born dead or retarded or crippled. And breeding in Treecats just isn't the answer. Oh, sweet Sun be praised, not only new blood, but farspeak blood at that!"

Milo's exasperation was transmitted with his thought. "That's all very well, Aldora, but it will wait, there are other matters which will not! First of all, I managed to take one of the witchmen alive. Tell Mara that he says his name is William Gold and that he was working under the name of *Kooreeos* Skiros. I want her to learn as much as she can about him from Kornblau, especially whether or not he customarily works with a partner. I need that information quickly too.

"Second, Gold appears to have some deviltry up his sleeve. I took a pistol—you know what that is, remember I described it to you once—away from him and who knows what else he has in circulation around here. In fact, I think that he was hinting that this hall was going to be reduced with explosives tomorrow!"

Beneath her warm blankets, Aldora's shapely body shuddered. "Sun grant not, Milo! What you have told me of those ancient terrors sounds horrible beyond imagining

. . . and what the *Song of Prophecy* tells of that long-ago time, the gods' monstrous death arrows, which obliterated whole, huge cities in fire and invisible death . . ."

"Now don't panic, girl!" Milo reproved. "I hardly think the whoresons would go so far as to use nuclear weapons, not with one or more of their own well within range and unprotected. But as I've often said before, I don't want to see the ancient technology reintroduced. I want this new world to develop its own.

"At any rate, I want you here as soon as possible, you and the troops. Knowing you, you've probably ridden ahead with most of the cavalry. Just how close are you? How much of a force is with you? And how far back is the main body?"

Beaming, "Just a moment," she threw off the blankets and padded the few steps to the small folding table. Disregarding the night chill which prickled every square inch of her bare skin, she extracted a map from a tooled leather case, unrolled it, and anchoring one end with the watch lantern, pored over it for a few moments. "About sixty-three kaiee, Milo, a little less than forty clanmiles. If I break camp at dawn, I can have my immediate force there by midafternoon. I've got only a little over twenty-seven hundred horsemen with me—two thousand kahtahfrahktoee, five hundred lancers, and two hundred of my bodyguard. The rest of the cavalry is with the infantry and the trains, and they're on the Traderoad, maybe two days behind us."

"Does your map show Morguhn Hall, Aldora?"

After a brief pause, "Yes, near a tributary to the river we just forded. Roughly nine kaiee north of Morguhnpolis and a little east, perhaps an hour less marching time . . . say we'll be there by early afternoon, then."

"No, not good enough," Milo retorted. "That still might be too late. Break camp now and be on the march within the hour."

She protested, "But Milo, both the men and the horses

are worn very thin, and many of the cats have had to be mounted. The entire force *needs* one good night's rest, if they're to be in any decent shape to fight tomorrow."

"It just can't be helped," he brusquely replied. "I want you here as soon as possible, for we're under siege even now—several thousands of them against a garrison of perhaps a hundred. True, most of the rebels are poorly armed rabble at best, but with the suspicion of Gold's wild card in the game . . . besides, I doubt your force will have to do any fighting when they get here. The mob we're facing have damn-all discipline and were very nearly routed when we beat off the first attack. Show them two-and-a-half thousand mounted Regulars, and chances are they'll scatter to every point of the compass."

Grudgingly, she acquiesced. "All right, all right, Milo, we'll march tonight. Can we use the roads?"

"It doesn't really matter, Aldora. Most of the rebels are here, and so too are most of the loyalists. A small party of Kindred, led by Clanbard Hail Morguhn is missing, but I've scant hope for them.

"It will have to be the Gafnee Drill, I suppose. Individuals or groups will be considered hostile until definitely proven to be friendly. Any who refuse to surrender immediately are to be slain. When you're within my farspeak range, let me know. Questions?"

"Yes. Should I send a galloper to the main column? Do you want them to force their marches as well?"

"It might not be a bad idea," he assented. "Tell Lukos to secure Kehnooryos Deskati—since it's the home city of that bastard Myros, it's probably rotten to the core with this rebellion. He's to kill or lock up everyone with even a *soupçon* of authority. As for those damned priests, it might be well if they all die while trying to escape. Then he's to camp there until sent for."

Aldora was an old campaigner and wasted no time. While she was donning her thick, soft cotton undergarments, she mindspoke the two squadron commanders of her kahtahfrahktoee (Bili would have called such troops "dragoons"), the Subkeeleeohstos of the lancers, and the captain of her bodyguard. While still she was lacing leather shirt to leatherfaced canvas breeches, bugles commenced to blare. Then two of her horse archers entered the tent. Without a word, one began to repack her saddlebags and roll her blankets, while the other assisted her into boots and cuirass. He cinched the dirk belt with its depending skirt of mail round her slender waist, then thrust the heavy dirk into its frog, buckled the brassarts about her upper arms and the shoulder pieces above them. When the palettes protecting her armpits were in place, he deftly arranged the long ebon hair into two thick braids and lapped them over the crown of her small head, Horseclans-fashion, to provide helmet padding. Once her neck and throat were wound with several thicknesses of absorbent cotton cloth, a gorget of Pitzburk was buckled on.

She drew on her gold-stitched gauntlets while the spearman was adjusting her wide baldric from which was suspended her ancient Horseclans saber.

Then the archer spoke his first words. "Which helm, My Lady?"

She shrugged. "The Cat, I suppose."

The first archer was securing the last of her gear to her charger's saddle as she strode from her tent. She was barely in that saddle before the tent had been struck. Thirty minutes after the cessation of the farspeak conversation, her squadrons were on the move, light cavalry and Prairie Cats screening van and flanks.

Arrived upon the walls, Bili did not wonder that *Komees* Djeen had called out the garrison, for all the watchfires down by the creek were blazing, throwing clouds of red, winking sparks high into the black moonless sky. Countless dark forms scurried in and out of the rings of firelight, while a medley of shouts, the roll of drums, neighs of horses, ceaseless hammerings, and the occasional creakings of ungreased axles all blended into waves of sound which rolled up the hill and lapped against the walls.

When Bili joined the *Komees* and Captain Raikuh atop the corner tower closest to the enemy camp, the old man shook his helmeted head. "I don't know now. Possibly I erred in taking you all from your food, but when those bastards started milling about like flies on a dungheap, my first thought was that somehow or other that mob had been persuaded to launch a night assault. but they appear to be making no efforts to form up, so . . ."

"Ho, Chief Bili," Hwahltuh Sanderz clambered up to the aerie, armed with dirk, saber, light axe, hornbow, and no less than three cases of arrows. Grinning happily he said, "My kin are all in the places Subchief Djeen said was best. Now when do we fight? Will it be soon, Kinsman?"

The old *Komees* frowned and shrugged. "Maybe yes, maybe no, Chief Hwahltuh. All we can be certain of is that something unusual *is* going on down there. It can't be the arrival of the rebels' siege train, for their engines—such as the slapdash, jerry-built contraptions are!—rolled in at twilight, along with their tents and baggage. I'll tell you all, it sounds to me like reinforcements coming into camp, which would also account for all the hubbub round about the commander's pavilion."

"But where, My Lords," asked Captain Raikuh, "would Lord Myros get more troops? Not in this Duchy certainly. Now were this the Middle Kingdoms, any one or more of your neighbor lords could well be bringing his men in to augment whichever side offered the most in the way of land or loot, but . . ."

"Your pardon, Captain," Bili interrupted. "There's but one way to find out the truth of what's causing the rebels to so bestir themselves, when they should be licking their wounds and getting ready to die tomorrow."

"Now, hold!" snapped *Komees* Djeen. "I agree, a sortie may be just the thing, especially if we can capture an officer or priest alive. But I'll not see *you* leading that sortie, *Thoheeks* Biji! If that's what you had in mind, think you you've not yet fully recovered from your wounds of that affray at the bridge. Besides, you're Chief now. It's not your place to lead attacks. You're the clan's strategist, to use army terminology; the Tahneest and the Subchiefs are the tacticians. Tahneest Djehf may not own your skill with that overgrown axe you fancy, but he's a stark warrior for all that, and he's a sound head on his shoulders. I've conversed with him—I know!"

Bili's left hand, gripping his swordhilt, was the only visible strain in his demeanor; its knuckles shone white as snow. However, when he spoke his voice was controlled, though steely-cold as a drawn blade. "*Komees* Djeen, I've deferred to your wisdom and experience in most aspects of warfare, as should all men here, for your knowledge of combats and sieges and weapons is truly encyclopedic. But if you think that on your word alone I'm going to climb up on the shelf and allow my brother or other men to do my fighting for me, you have seriously misjudged both my mettle and your own importance!"

Hwahltuh Sanderz laid his hand on Bili's rigid forearm. "Kinsman Chief, your words make my heart warm. From what I had seen riding through the lands south of here, I had thought that courage and honor and love of fighting had been bred out of all the eastern Kindred. But in you, I see I was mistaken. You eat Dirtman food and you wash too much, true, but for all that you live to the Law."

Then the wiry little Chief turned to the *Komees,* saying reprovingly, "Subchief Djeen, you give shameful advice to your Chief. He is Chief and son of a Chief. As such, *his* duty under The Law is to lead his clan, while *your* duty under The Law is to follow him. The *Couplets of The Law* say:

For it is meet the old should teach the young
Of how the bow be drawn, the saber swung.

"You are far older than Chief Bili, even older than am I. So why is it that you needs must be instructed in your proper duty?"

Komees Djeen gritted his teeth, painfully swallowing the rejoinder he would have loved to but dared not make. These wild Horseclansmen were well known both for inordinate pride and the quick tempers of stud bulls. One wrong word from him, he knew, and the feisty little bastard's steel would be out and the fat would be in the fire for fair. So he chose his words, framing his answer with exacting care.

"Chief Hwahltuh, the Law which was given the Sacred Ancestors by the Undying God Milo was formulated centuries ago for a race of man. They were for long the very salvation of that race. But, Chief Hwahltuh, they were drafted to fit the needs of a specific lifestyle. Clan Morguhn and the other forty-one clans trekked and fought their way to the sea under that Law. Their swords and their Courage and the Law sustained them through thousands of kaiee of hostile country, filled with savage beasts and bloodthirsty peoples.

"But look about you, Chief Hwahltuh, the descendants of those Horseclansmen are no longer nomads. They still breed horses and cattle, sheep and goats, some still mindspeak and hunt game, but they have adapted to a settled way of life. They have interbred with the Ehleenoee, who were the previous lords of these lands, with mountain folk and with men and women from the northern principalities.

"Over the generations since the Coming of the Horseclans, we are become a different race from those whose swords hacked their marks of ownership onto duchies such as this one. As we changed racially, so too did our laws and our customs. They had to, else we would have remained but a host of barbarians, squatting amidst the charred ruins of a once civilized land.

"The number of these changes of the Law is legion, but the change which here affects us is this: Our Clan Chief is expected to be ruler, administrator, judge. It is thought good for him to be an experienced warrior, aggressive and unafraid to see blood spilled or to have swords drawn when such be necessary, and to know warfare well. But it is frowned upon, and highly unusual, for a Chief to lead into actual combat, for the loss of a good Chief would be crushing. So while the Chief plans the movements of his forces, it is the function of the Tahneest to see that those plans are carried out—it is almost the only function of the Clan Tahneest, in our society.

"Bili has been Chief for less than a day, Chief Hwahltuh. Further, for the last ten years he dwelt in a distant and alien land. That he now recalls as much as he does of our laws and customs is in itself amazing and indicative of his rare mental abilities and the priceless value of his Chieftainship in years to come. I feel sure that he will prove the best Morguhn of Morguhn within memory, if I and the others can keep him alive.

"Now Bili's uncle, who was Tahneest under his father, is dead, murdered by those would-be soldiers down there. Djehf Morguhn, who as Bili's oldest brother is now Tahneest, lacks our Bili's phenomenal memory, so remembers less than he. Under these conditions, it should be the function of Clanbard Hail to cleave to the new Chief's side, instructing and counseling him until he is conversant with all aspects of his new position, but I fear that poor Hail too has gone to Wind, so the Clanbard's task is fallen upon *Komees* Hari, *Vahrohnos* Spiros, and me, who are the senior Subchiefs.

"Chief Hwahltuh, Chief Bili's youthful impetuosity *must* be curbed, and the sooner the better. For a Chief who is ruled by his emotions, rather than by law and custom and considered judgment, is dangerous to the wellbeing of his clan!"

They left by way of rope ladders, down one of the darkest sections of wall, all except the two Cats, who simply jumped the—to them, piddling—fifteen feet. Djehf and Pawl Raikuh led a dozen hardboiled Freefighters, while Chief Hwahltuh and Subchief Mak Sanderz headed six of their best bowmen, *Komees* Djeen having flatly refused to permit any more of the valuable Horseclans archers to be risked—and Hwahltuh's temper be damned.

Several minutes later, Milo landed on the balls of his feet, his knees flexed to absorb the impact. After a deliberate roll, he came to a stop beside Whitetip, who had preceded him down the slope. In his own ears, the muted clashing of his armor had sounded loud as an alarum bell, but so tumultuous was the hurrah from the siege lines, that he doubted any had remarked upon his noise.

Gliding into a patch of more stygian darkness, he stood up and brushed at the ankle-length, black cassock which covered his armor. Dropping his helm but retaining the steel skullcap, he donned a flatcrowned, brimless hat of fine black felt. He gingerly patted and tugged at the false beard—full and black and square-cut—to see that it had not loosened during his descent from Morguhn Hall. After another pat to be sure that the jewelled, pectoral cross of Skiros/Gold still hung from his neck, he again crouched and trotted down toward the camp, paced by Whitetip.

They halted just beyond the light of a watchfire and Milo rapidly took in the scene spread before him. Far to his left, perhaps a hundred yards away, lay the pavilions of the officers and priests with several scores of figures clustered about the largest. Some of these figures held horses, some stood in groups talking earnestly, some scurried to and fro. Just as a party emerged from the big pavilion, Milo's attention was distracted by happenings nearer to hand.

A huge wain, drawn by two span of brawny white mules, trundled into the circle of red yellow light, conveyance and draft animals still wet and muddy from the ford. Two bawling, whip-wielding horsemen preceded it, mercilessly clearing a right of way by dint of pain and curses. Four mounted subpriests flanked the high-wheeled cart, a full priest drove the team, and a big man in the rich robes of a *Kooreeos* bestrode a fine, white-stockinged chestnut behind. On this last cleric's broad chest, the firelight was reflected in the jewels of a cross identical to that now worn by Milo.

Absently, the High-Lord fingered the cross, and under a finger, one of the jewels sank smoothly into its setting. The cross commenced a low, persistent buzzing then, and from its right arm, a rounded plastic cone popped out to dangle from a slender wire.

The mounted *Kooreeos* suddenly raised his cross to his lips, at the same time placing his right hand to his ear. His bearded lips moved and from a seemingly vast distance Milo heard a tinny voice, though he could make out no words.

Wonderingly, he brought his own big cross near his mouth. A tentative pull at the cone caused a bit more wire to emerge, just enough to allow him to insert the cone in his ear.

". . . dy? Where in hell are you?" The voice came in clearly. "These damned transceivers never have worked consistently. Those five-thumbed apes that Dumb-dumb Bob May has in Electronics Engineering—I doubt if any one of them can wipe their butts properly! Goldy? Goldy, can you hear me?"

Slurring his words, Milo answered, "Loud and clear."

"Have they still got you chained up in that cellar, Goldy?" demanded the voice, adding, "There's some sort of distortion in my reception, you sound odd."

Milo thought fast, then slurred his transmission even more. "No, ish not your shet. Get hit in mouf. Shwollen."

"Sadistic bastards!" snarled the other. "Well, we'll have you out of there soon, Goldy, just hold on. I've brought enough impact bombs to level a city, much less that molehill up there!"

Face still puffy and discolored from the beating cheerfully given him by the bodyguards of *Vahrohnos* Myros, a spike-bearded man Bili would have recognized as the enemy leader at the bridge fight sat in a small, ill-equpped tent with a couple of his subordinates, circulating a skin of inferior wine. Their minuscule condotta of professionals constituted the only reliable troops in the "army" and said professionals knew it, even if their employers affected to not know.

During the months that the three officers, their sergeants, and men had devoted to almost uniformly vain attempts to make soldiers of rabble, they had come to hate their students almost as much as they despised their mealy-mouthed, pennypinching employers. Now all of them—the officers in the sole tent they had been allowed, and the sergeants and men squatting about the fires—were softly chortling over various aspects of the late afternoon's abortive assault and trading gallows-humorous speculations on exactly what would transpire when next their "comrades in arms" could be beaten or chivvied up the hill to once more face the tough little band within Morguhn Hall.

"If I thought for even one moment—" the captain moved his lips as little as possible and his words hissed through the void created by the recent loss of a couple of front teeth. "—that those feisty bastards up there stood even an outside chance of winning, of holding off this stinking mob . . ."

The younger of the two lieutenants slowly nodded. "I think that most of us feel just that way too. The

Thoheeks is all man and he commands men. We're here surrounded by a vast herd of rooting swine!"

"We'll be smart not to talk what-all we feels," put in the older lieutenant brusquely. "How do we know who's a-listnin'? And I sure-lord don't wanta be the one as is caught plottin' against the Vahrohnos! 'Sides, the reinforcements what come in tonight and the others what'll be here t'morra from *Thoheekseen* Vawn, they all knows what it is to win, so they'll really fight. And the half a hunnerd the *Thoheeks* is got jest ain't enough to hol' thet place aginst no real assault."

The younger lieutenant assumed an exaggeratedly sanctimonious pose and expression, while his voice mocked the emoting tones of a priest. "And forget you not, Brothers in God, we fight not for base gold, but for The True Faith; not for crass loot, but for our souls' salvation!"

The captain made a rude noise and instantly regretted the pain it brought to his battered face.

"Mebbe!" snorted the other lieutenant. "But me, I don't give a cowpat fer them furfaces and alla this here religious hogwash!" He slapped his wellworn hilt. "You guys is Ehleenee. Well I ain't, and Uncle Sharptooth here. He's the onlies' deesunt god fer a soljer. And when I fights, by cracky I fights for loot!"

"Yes," agreed the younger. "Loot is the reason most soldiers fight. But there is honor, as well. The Steel God of you barbarians demands that, above all."

The spikebeard took another long draught of the foul wine, then commented, "Well, it's scant honor any of us will bear from this campaign. I thought this was to be an honest civil war when I took gold and swore my oath and set about recruiting most of you. *Fah!* And here we are, helping a lunatic pervert and a gaggle of fanatic priests and a gang of gallows-bait commoners murder their rightful lords. We . . . Now what in thunder has got into the horses?"

Although theirs was but a small picketline, a certain

amount of noise was a normal occurrence throughout any night, for these were all high-spirited warhorses, many of them uncut stallions and all bred and trained to fight. Of course, it was standard operating procedure in any war-camp that mares were picketed well away from full horses, but even so random bites and the occasional shrill combat were not uncommon. So the veteran cavalrymen had ignored the stampings and snortings and whinnyings, and even the first scream or two.

But now there had erupted a veritable chorus of high-pitched screams, screams not of rage but fear! The entire length of the horselines were vocalizing unmistakable terror. Nostrils dilated and eyes rolling whitely, they reared and jerked at the restraints without visible cause.

Abruptly, a picketline went down and twoscore of the fear-mad chargers fled mindlessly through the crowded camp, trampling or savaging all who sought to halt them! And unseen in the darkness and confusion, Lover-of-water and young Steelclaws loped away toward their next assignment, leaving Myros's tiny cavalry-arm in utter chaos.

But the cavalry encampment was concealed from the sight of the headquarters area by an undulation of the terrain. The tumult was effectively swallowed by distance and the general racket of the intervening camps. It was not until screams of mortal agony smote their ears that some score of officers and priests came boiling out of Myros's pavilion, the men of Vawn tired and worn by their long, forced march and those of Morguhn all in some measure tiddly of a surfeit of the *Vahrohnos's* strong wines.

By then it was too late. Dozens of Sanderz firearrows had set the wagons and the stores and most of the newly assembled war engines ablaze. Out of the darkness, swarms of black-lacquered shafts buzzed, bearing the sting of death to any and all who sought to subdue the blazes. A cask of strong cordial in one of the wagons exploded with a dull boom, showering glowing sparks and bits of flaming wood onto the fringes of the closely grouped officers' tents. The blue and green flames from the waterproofed canvas were soon rising higher and hotter than the red and yellow conflagration of the siege train.

While the knot of temporal and spiritual leaders reeled in exhausted or drunken confusion, shouting meaningless or contradictory orders to servants or horseholders or empty air, a volley of heavy, well-aimed darts thudded in among them. A second volley took out most of the horseholders. Then a horde of coal black, demonic figures were among the terrified survivors, their swords and sabers and light axes hacking a wide swath of bloody ruin.

Myros had donned his ornate dress armor for the purpose of meeting his incoming allies, but the armor of his officers still lay within his pavilion; so they and the unarmed priests had suffered most heavily from the darts. The armed and armored officers of Vawn valiantly drew their steel and at least slowed the attackers. The *Vahrohnos* tore a target from the deathgrip of an officer whose eyesocket sprouted two feet of dartshaft, then trotted over with naked sword to take his place amongst the dwindling ranks of the Vawnee.

Those officers and priests not dead or dying fled in every direction, their terrified shrieks lost in the cacaphony of the burning camps. For his own part, "Captain" Nathos Evrehos, the goldsmith-moneylender, ran sobbing into the inky void, his face streaked with his tears and his legs streaked with his dung.

"But, 'm not inna hall," slurred Milo into the pectoral cross. "Shcaped."

"Capital, Goldy!" crowed the mounted *Kooreeos,* his broad grin distinct from where Milo stood. "Capital! Where are you, now?"

Whitetip's farspeak had reached first the familiar mind of Rik Sanderz, and it was that young clansman and one of his kin who opened the rear gates that Milo might drive the mules and the heavy burden they drew—now increased by the weight of the unconscious *Kooreeos* of Vawn. The handsome chestnut, captivated by Milo's mindspeak, trotted along behind the wain. The faces of the two clansmen were wreathed in grins at the Bard's successful exploit.

But there was no hint of a smile on the hard face of the *Thoheeks,* only restrained ferocity. Not even the warm glow of the torches could thaw the icy stare which bored into the blackrobed back, as Milo descended from the lofty driver's seat and ripped off the hot, itchy "beard."

Bili's words were clipped and cold rage was in his voice. "Bard Klairuhnz, I assigned you to a critically important post. You saw fit to desert that post. There is but one fitting punishment for such an action at so grave a time as the present." His huge axe was gripped in his right hand and with his left he drew his dirk, saying, "You once fought well and faithfully for me, Kinsman, so I now allow you a choice. Will I take your head with my axe or heart-thrust you with the dirk?"

The corner of Milo's eye caught a stiff flickering of a white-tipped tail, as the great feline crouched and tensed to spring. "No!" he beamed urgently. "Let be, Cat-brother. This is as quick a way as any to confirm to the lad my true identity."

"The dirk, I think, Lord Bili," answered Milo, gravely. "But, for that, I must remove my brigandine."

At that, he doffed the robe and cross, loosened the crotch strap, grasped the hem of the steel-lined garment, and started to pull it over his head. In a blur of movement, Bili tossed axe to left and dirk to right hand, and his hard, true, straight-armed thrust thudded home between Milo's ribs, the force of the blow slamming him back against the high wheel of the wain.

Rik and the other Sanderz man gripped their sun medallions, but took in the deed with impassive faces. For Bili was a Chief and Bard Klairuhnz apparently had been his oathman. He had not attempted to dissuade his Chief, nor to stave off the execution, so obviously had he deemed death his just punishment. Their own Chief had admonished them that they must all bide by the ways of this land. Besides, they recognized their unpleasant affair to be none of Clan Sanderz's business.

Komees Djeen's limping run brought him to his young lord's side just as the dirk came free with an obscene, sucking pop, and blood, glistening black in the torchlight, gushed forth to soak the shirt above the wound.

"You damned thick-skulled young fool!" snarled the old man, furiously jerking Bili about. "You're not in Harzburk, dammit, what you've just done is murder! You . . . *Sun and Wind!*" His contorted, livid features suddenly slackened and blanched to the hue of curds, while his faded-blue eye seemed about to spring from its socket.

Bili whirled around, then unconsciously stepped back, his own eyes flitting back and forth between his blood-slimed dirk and his "victim."

Milo finished pulling the brigandine over his head and with it the blue black wig which had covered his own, close-cropped grey-and-black hair. He smiled fleetingly at the stunned *Thoheeks,* then inserted a forefinger into first one cheek, then the other, wincing as he tore loose lumpy strips of some substance which had served to alter the shape of his face.

Then the "dead man" pulled off his shirt and Bili could see that the wide wound his blade had inflicted had almost ceased to bleed. His confused brain spun frenetically, registering what it saw, yet knowing that such could not be . . . unless . . .

Komees Djeen's sword came from its case in one smooth movement; then its hilt crashed against his breastplate in a stiff, military salute, as he croaked, "My Lord, My Dear Lord . . .!"

Almost simultaneously did two Sanderz sabers come

out to render Horseclan honors, while two awestruck voices murmured, "*God Milo!*"

It was nearly an hour more before the sortiers straggled back to the hall. Although they had failed to capture any officer or priest, they had retired in good order, bearing with them both their wounded and their dead. But even when the last of them were sprawled gasping within the walls, the clash of arms still sounded from the creekside camps, as leaderless bands of hopelessly bewildered men took similar bands for the enemy in the darkness between fires. And the murderous chaos went on until the first roseate streaks of dawn were tinting the eastern sky.

When the coppery vanguard of Sacred Sun breasted the horizon, most of the garrison of the beleaguered hall gathered in the rear courtyard. While Clanbard Gil sang first *The Lament of Morguhn*, then *The Lament of Sanderz*, the bodies were borne from indoors in stately procession, laid upon the enlarged pyre, and torches were set to its four corners by Bili, Spiros, Hwahltuh, and Raikuh.

Slowly at first, then ever more rapidly, the tongues of flame took hold and crept higher and higher, then began to nibble at the pitch-soaked boards whereon lay the seven corpses. Bili gazed woodenly but once more upon the faces of his kin and those who had fought for him, and stepped back as the heat became uncomfortable.

The column of smoke rose up and up and up, high into the pale-blue dawning sky, until a high-altitude current struck it powerfully and sent its tendrils roiling away to the west.

Hwahltuh and his clansmen stood bunched together, touching one another for comfort, whilst unashamed tears streaked their faces—tears not only for the losses of two loved kinsmen, but for pride that the smoke of Sanderz men should be borne to the Home of Sacred Wind in company with that of a Chief and his brave son.

The Freefighters stood at attention behind their captain, with no need to force the appearance of emotionlessness, for—like eating, drinking, wenching, gambling, and fighting—death was but another facet of the existence of a professional soldier.

Despite himself, old *Komees* Djeen, standing ramrod-stiff at Milo's left rear, felt moisture creeping from his eye and down the folds and puckers and wrinkles of his leathery cheek. For his part *Vahrohnos* Spiros wept as openly as the Sanderz men.

Bili was the first upon the walls when the tower watch winded the alarm bugle. But he could see nothing other than individuals and small groups shuffling about the charred and bloody wreckage of the rebel encampments. So he quickly ascended the nearest tower. And there he did not need the guard's pointing spear to show him.

When the leading elements of Confederation cavalry were reported by the Vawnee scouts, the few remaining officers betook themselves to the commander's pavilion, but it stood empty and stripped of all small valuables. *Vahrohnos* Myros, the senior subpriest, Rikos, and their guards were nowhere to be found! As the highest ranking noble remaining, *Vahrohneeskos* Drehkos Daiviz found himself in command of the self-battered siege forces.

If no soldier, Drehkos was at least a good administrator; so after sending the scouts back to their posts with orders to keep him informed of the progress of the leading force and the approximate size of the main element, he assembled such staff as was available and commenced a riding tour of the wrecked, wretched camps to assess just what he was in command of. Within the hour, he had ordered and was supervising immediate and rapid withdrawal to Morguhnpolis!

Leaning between the merlons, Bili shouted down to the Freefighter bugler, "You, trooper! Sound first the Officers' Call, then the Assembly!"

The Freefighter had not completed the first call ere the young *Thoheeks* was down from the tower and racing along the wallwalk toward the hall. The large central chamber was still filling up when he arrived, buckling on his gorget, the straps of his hastily donned cuirass dangling loose. As he gained the dais and strode to his place at the high table, *Komees* Djeen stumped up to confront him, angrily demanding:

"Now just what in hell do you think you're up to? Have you no respect for the rites due your father and the honors for your poor, brave brother?"

"Who would not be dead, remember, had I not, against my better judgment, heeded your overly cautious advice and given into his leadership the raid I planned and should have led!" Ice crackled in Bili's voice and stare, and his tone brooked no argument. "Now *you* heed *me*, Lord Djeen, and heed me well, for I shall not repeat my words! You are a man grown old in war and there is much I may learn from you, but I will learn when and as I *wish* to learn, not at *your* pleasure!

"Sacred Sun has made of me your rightful lord, not the reverse. Do not delude yourself into the belief that I will longer tolerate your browbeating. In the future, you will either obey my orders, or you have my leave to forthwith depart my presence! I tell you this before the face of Him who is the Ancient God of our ancestors and present overlord of us all.

"I know that you have meant well and that command is become habitual with you, but you have left me no choice, Lord Djeen. You must realize that although you are a Count and have been a General, *I* am a Duke and, my age notwithstanding, your temporal superior!

"Am I understood, Lord Djeen?"

"Perfectly, My Lord *Thoheeks*." The *Komees*'s words came as stiff as his military posture, but his eye showed grudging respect. "I await your orders."

"Very good," Bili nodded, then signed Raikuh's lieutenant to do up the loose straps of his armor while he spoke on. "Our erstwhile besiegers are breaking camp and withdrawing in some haste. Even as I quitted the watchtower, a large body of cavalry forded the creek and rode west, toward Morguhnpolis, I assume. Without horsemen to protect them, those rebel foot will be ripe for the slaughter and I mean to butcher me as many as I can lay axe to.

"You and Kinsman Sami will again have command of the hall. I will leave you Kinsman Vaskos, the six walking wounded, and your personal Freefighters."

Wordlessly, the old Strahteegos saluted, turned about, and stumped off, trailed by Vaskos and the castellan.

"Chief Hwahltuh, Captain Raikuh, get your men armed and mounted. I'll expect the column to be formed up and ready in fifteen minutes."

The little Chief whooped delightedly, vaulted the table, and sped toward the door, his shouting, laughing clansmen close behind him. Raikuh nodded his acknowledgment and saluted, but even he could not repress a grin.

Komees Hari stepped forward. "Bili . . . uh, My Lord *Thoheeks*, I may be old, but . . ."

Bili smiled warmly. "But you're not too old to swing a sword, eh? I had no thought of leaving you and our other Kinsmen behind, Lord Hari. It is only because he is wounded that I ordered your son to remain. But all of you hurry and get armed, for I want no unnecessary delay. I want to rout those bastards!"

When the nobles were gone, only Milo and Master Ahlee remained with Bili on the dais. "And I?" inquired the whiterobed physician. "What would the Lord *Thoheeks* have me to do?"

Bili smiled again. "Whatever you wish, Lord Ahlee, for you have served me and my House well. I know you to be a stark warrior, for all that you profess to be a man of peace. You may remain with your patients or you may ride with me."

Ahlee's gentle smile answered Bili's. "Young Eeshmaheel is become as accomplished a physician as am I.

Indeed, he already has a 'volunteer apprentice,' so the wounded here can receive no better care from me. I had long forgotten how exhilarating is combat. I will fetch my blade and see to my horse."

"And me, Bili?" inquired Milo.

The smile slipped from the young *Thoheeks*' face. "Who am I to give orders to My Lord?" he answered uncomfortably, the memory of his attempt to execute this more-than-man still painfully fresh in his mind.

"No, Bili," Milo mindspoke. "Put that from your thoughts. I knew your intention and could easily have stopped you, had I so desired.

"But that was last night. May I ride with your force this morning?"

"Any sound horse in my stables is yours, My Lord," Bili silently assured him. "I will be most honored to do whatever the High-Lord commands."

Milo grinned. "Remember that promise, Bili; for are you truly that which I believe you to be. I have great plans for you.

"But for now, for a little while longer, think of me only as your distant-Kinsman Klairuhnz, and command me as you would him. You see, young Bili, the life of a High-Lord is often boring, and I must return to that life soon enough.

"Now," he smiled, "shall we go and see if that witch-man's big chestnut is the charger he claims to be?"

THE DOSADI EXPERIMENT

Frank Herbert

From the author of *DUNE*

THE DOSADI EXPERIMENT: Frank Herbert's new novel, a swirling, vividly complex story set on the most alien and challenging world he has yet created – a brutal prison planet where 850 million beings are confined in 40 square kilometres.

THE DOSADI EXPERIMENT: a stunning evocation of alien cultures, and of an experiment so monstrous it threatens the entire galaxy.

'Totally credible and told with an ease which belies an extraordinary control over the genre' *The Times*

'J. R. R. Tolkien and C. S. Lewis are not in Mr Herbert's inventive league . . . The range is staggering . . . Splendid entertainment, with moral sinew and an astonishing romance' *New York Times*

Science Fiction
0 7088 8035 5